Appalachian Holidays

An Anthology of Stories, Poetry &
Art Celebrating Fall, Thanksgiving, and
Christmas in the Mountains

Appalachian Creators

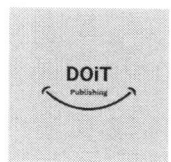

DOIT PUBLISHING, LLC

Paperback ISBN: 978-1-958685-06-8

eBook ISBN: 978-1-958685-08-2

Hardback ISBN: 978-1-958685-07-5

DISCLAIMER

This anthology is a work of creative expression. While inspired by Appalachian culture, traditions, and seasonal celebrations, all characters, events, and art portrayed in these stories are either products of the authors' imaginations or are used fictitiously, or not.

All exaggerations of truth (an Appalachian tradition) are purely coincidental or heavily embellished for entertainment purposes. Any resemblance to actual persons, living or deceased (or somewhere in between), or real-life feasts, or family feuds is purely coincidental (but not entirely impossible).

The editors, artists, and publishers make no claims regarding the historical accuracy or emotional preparedness of the reader for the contents described within. Readers are advised not to attempt any holiday stunts mentioned herein without proper supervision, common sense, or a note from a responsible elder.

No pumpkins, turkeys, or Christmas trees were harmed during the making of this book — though a few may have been slightly traumatized.

Read with joy, laugh with love, and please enjoy our renditions of memories of the holiday season.

DEDICATION

To the Possum who Crashed our Late October Picnic — You were the surprise guest and the main course.

To the Turkey who escaped Thanksgiving Dinner and became a Local Legend. — Run free, Giblet.

To Everyone who's ever Decorated a Tractor for Christmas — you're the reason Santa knows we mean business in Appalachia.

For Granny, who puts Moonshine in the Eggnog and Jesus in everything else.

To my cousin Daryl, who tried to deep-fry a snowman. He's fine now.

To the Readers of our Anthology – Now your Life is Complete.

CONTENTS

Introduction

Welcome to our Anthology

... of Holiday Reflections, Mountain Folklore, and Artistic Expressions.

Nestled in the misty valleys and snow-dusted ridges of the Appalachian Mountains lies a world where every season tells a story.

Appalachian Holidays is a delightful, entertaining, and at times haunting anthology that celebrates the spirit, struggle, and beauty of life in the mountains during the last holidays of the year.

This rich collection brings together short stories, poetry, artwork, fiction, and true accounts from writers and artists who have lived, loved, and remembered the Appalachian way of life.

WHO WE ARE

The Appalachian Mountains span over 2,000 miles across the eastern and northeastern parts of the United States and into eastern Canada. Coincidentally, 2,000 species of plants grow along the Appalachian Mountain range, AND the Appalachian trail is just over 2,000 miles long.

Dang. There's no conclusion here; just sharing. Likewise, we believe you'll find 2,000 reasons to enjoy and share the prose, memories, and art in the following pages. Incidentally, none of the stories are over 2,000 words.

The oldest mountain range in North America, The Appalachian Mountains have embraced generations of inventive and resilient people who created a unique culture filled with stories, history, imagination, and music. Over the years, we have entertained ourselves and others by sharing folklore, legends, customs, and crafts. Here we go again – in this anthology.

In the Appalachian region of Southwest Virginia there exists a diverse group of humans who habitually congregate to share knowledge, offer encouragement, and experience the success and failure of one another's quests in open-hearted and friendly discussion. We call ourselves Persiflage Writers.

PERSIFLAGE means frivolous conversation and bantering talk or writing with light raillery and teasing. Now you know a new word.

Dan Smith, founder of the Roanoke Regional Writers Conference, created our Persiflage community, and we have become an Appalachian family of sorts. Dan has assembled a gathering of minds who appreciate and cherish the variety of perspectives we share. His generous spirit of inspiring and encouraging creativity has kindled growth and motivation in countless aspiring and successful creators from every walk of life.

His influence exemplifies the enduring bonds of kinship that reflect the unique culture of our Appalachian Mountains.

Kathie Dickenson, a Persiflage writer, dedicated count-less hours to edit and forward the contributions here-in. Kathie is the best editor I've ever known. She can gently blast a dangling participle or intrusive comma from a mountain-side tree stand with the precision of a 16-yr-old whose mama taught 'em to shoot. And we appreciate that. I think it gives her joy.

Each piece in the following pages honors the traditions, celebrations, and memories that infuse Appalachian Holidays with a reverence for those simple joys of life.

Some of our tales will make you laugh. Some will chill you to the bone; others will warm your heart, or move you to tears.

Our Anthology is more than a collection of holiday ren-derings—it's a tapestry of heart, humor, and heritage woven from the voices of Appalachia.

~ Debbie Seagle

Bryan Skinnell

FICTION

FALL PUMPKIN   by Linda Thomas

Community Theater

Lori D'Angelo

She knew how she was supposed to feel. She had seen this play before. Every Christmas. At a theater just out-side of Lexington. With her mother and her mother's friend who was really more than a friend. But she pre-tended not to understand. Being willfully ignorant was what kept the world running. Because, if we admitted the truth about anything, then how were we supposed to go on?

Usually, as Ebenezer Scrooge came out and laughed and thanked his lucky stars that he had not missed Christ-mas, that he would not die alone, and some sketchy woman wouldn't steal his belongings because he was kind, Becca wanted to cry, and not tears of joy.

At least Miser Scrooge was kind of fun. And Christmas celebrations with the spending expectations that grew

more and more ridiculous each year had become anything other than fun.

It was December 23rd, and she still had 15 people to
buy for:

- Jerry, her kindly but hard-to-buy-for boss (like
  what message did she want to send?) and Jane,
  her annoying "I do soooo much volunteering"
  coworker who thought that instead of gifts
  everyone should donate to the charity of HER
  choice.

- Her mother and her mother's friend (did she
  really have to buy for him?).

- Her father who would return whatever she got
  him no matter how nice or thoughtful. He was
  a little Scroogy with his "I don't need anything"
  attitude.

- Her current boyfriend, Joe.

- Her ex-boyfriend Matthew, who insisted on
  meeting her for pie at some old people's diner
  every Christmas Eve. Afterward, they kissed for
  old times' sake and auld lang syne and pretended like it didn't count because mistletoe.

After Matthew, the list got even more weirdly complicat-
ed. Not only did she have to buy for her mother's man
friend who her mother wished was her lover, but they
were both too repressed to do anything other than hold
each other's hands. She also had to buy for his daughter,
who was a really sweet kid. Becca actually sort of liked
her even though she thought her dad was kind of a shit-
head. The girl, who had the unfortunate modern name
Brionna, liked to do magic tricks and wear a black cape.
She was young enough that her personality hadn't yet
been quashed by teenage cultural uniformity where all

the girls liked the same shows, wore the same clothes, and talked about the same boring boys.

There was also her Great Aunt Margaret, who had lived longer than anyone she thought could or should. Her cramped apartment was a monument to old newspapers and shot glass collections. Becca was tempted to steal some glasses to see if old Margaret would notice or care. But she didn't because she had a certain respect for a woman who insisted on living alone and not giving a shit. Margaret was among the easiest to buy for. She liked Kentucky bourbon, and when Becca hopped over with a bottle, Margaret always shared. And they drank it down and watched It's a Wonderful Life until they both laugh-cried. Margaret liked librarian Mary's character the most. Becca liked Clarence because he was such a hapless angel, but he hung in there. He really had some Rooster Cogburn grit. So much of life, Becca thought, was just about showing up and outwaiting everyone else.

Like seriously, why couldn't Scrooge have been like yeah, my sister was good and nice and all, but she's dead. Like Billy Joel said (admittedly Scrooge would not have heard of Billy Joel), "Only the good die young."

Becca could have imagined a much more fun version of A Christmas Carol where Scrooge did the Monster Mash with Jacob Marley and the Ghost of Christmas Past and Present (Present did seem like a party animal). Who knows, maybe even Mr. Creepy Grim Reaper Christmas Future could have joined in? Would he make that weird screechy movie sound effect noise even when he danced?

Tonight, her theater buddy was not her mother and her mother's man friend (thank God). Luckily, (okay also not so luckily), man friend's daughter had gotten sick (she wasn't dying or anything, so it was okay), and he had to miss the annual outing with Becca and her mother.

Becca's mother was morose, and she refused to go without him. She wheezed pathetically like freakin' Tiny Tim, "You go, have fun, without me."

"Okay," Becca had said almost too cheerily, "I will." Her mom's man friend reminded Becca of Buddy the Elf's elf dad, played by Bob Newhart, so kind and old and asexual. He was like a frog or something. And not the into prince kind.

Becca had these tickets and no date. And she wasn't about to drag Joe. They hadn't yet tried to include each other in their lame yearly half-hearted holiday traditions. Her rendezvous with Matthew was a once a year only at that diner kind of thing. And her Great Aunt Margaret didn't like leaving the apartment complex.

So, there was Becca and the tickets. And she didn't feel like going alone. But, to spite her mother, and so the tickets didn't go to waste, she was going.

Her boss, Jerry, had worked at the office for what seemed like 80,000 years. But it was maybe more like 10. And while Becca was between things, he was settled. This was his job. This was his life. He had two divorces and maybe shared custody of a dog behind him. Becca wasn't really sure. She didn't keep up on all the workplace drama. She was just there to kill days and make money until she figured out her true purpose in life. She was beginning to wonder if she had one. Her mother was a teacher and not the 7 to 3 kind. She was one of those women who oozed education from every pore, like she had never wanted to be anything else. As if she had emerged from the womb and picked up a pencil, eraser, and gradebook, and that was that.

Jerry wasn't unattractive or attractive. He was just generic boss man. But maybe it was all the light and darkness that made her see him differently that night. When Scrooge was trying to avoid his grave fate, Becca slowly eased her hand over to Jerry's armrest and into his personal space. Casually, carefully, she found his fingers. And she gripped them hard. She released the pressure a little to see what he would do. He held her hand steadily, not too tight and not too loose, but possessively, not letting go.

Becca was intrigued. She couldn't wait for Scrooge to shut up about the joy of Christmas and yet part of her wanted him to keep going on and on so she could keep on holding Jerry's hand. After the second bow and the obligatory community theater standing ovation, he took his coat and put it protectively around her shoulders, quiet as the Ghost of Christmas Future but less ominous. Outside, her hands were getting cold. So, he offered her his sleek black gloves, and did she want a ride home? She nodded, heart pounding. She had ridden in his car before. What was it? A Subaru? A station wagon? A family vehicle for a man without a family. The back was roomy. And when they got inside, they, like Scrooge, wasted no time, as if the ghosts had given them a second chance. Becca ignored the vibrating of her cell phone. She had silenced it for the play. Was it Mom, or Joe, or Dad? She really didn't care.

Afterward, breathless, she didn't know what to say, but something seemed called for. And it didn't seem like that something was Okay, then! See you Monday at 8 am. Still struggling for words, she reached over and kissed him, and he kissed her back and the kiss was long and slow and tender.

"Spirit," she asked, "is this for real now?"

He laughed gently. And heartily. And she teased him in a bad British accent, "Shall we have a Christmas feast?"

"I think we just did," he said.

She was both excited and uncertain. "But was it all just a dream?" she asked. "And, if so, what lesson am I supposed to learn?"

"I think the lesson's fairly obvious," he said. And she waited for him to explain. "If a beautiful young woman asks you to accompany her to a play, take her."

"And then?"

"Buy her the best turkey?"

"What if she doesn't want a turkey?"

"What does she want?" he asked her seriously.

"What if she doesn't know?"

"Offer to help her figure it out. Would she like that?"

"She's not sure. She's surprised," she said. "Because she didn't realize how much she liked you or any of this. She thought maybe this was just a phase she was passing through while you were set and settled."

"Hm," he said. "What if she was wrong?"

"Maybe ghosts can visit her and help her see the error of her ways? Or . . ."

"Or what?"

"Fun and kisses, and can I just ask you one favor?"

"What?" he asked.

"Can you please not let Jane choose the charity?"

He laughed again then, and she thought the sound was musical, like the cheerful mirth of the Ghost of Christmas Present.

"Hmm," she said, "this could go one of two ways. You leave me for the love of money, or you could marry me, and we have perfect kids but be threadbare poor."

"Or maybe there's a third, less 19th century option," he suggested. "Like you could do what you want to do and be what you want to be, and we could still keep in touch and be friends whether or not we ..."

"Hey, you're ruining my Dickensian Christmas," she said.

"Okay," he said, "what if I do this instead," and he kissed her long and hard and she told him about Joe and Matthew and the diner and her mom and her mom's man friend and his not half bad kid and her dad and how he never liked any of the presents she bought him and about drinking bourbon with Margaret. "That," she admitted, "is my favorite Christmas tradition. The rest I could take or leave."

He leaned over and kissed her again, slow and gentle. She felt warm and young and happy. "This," she said, "this I could get used to. Should we make it annual?"

"Or," he proposed carefully, "we could keep Christmas every day."

"That," she said, "I might like. Let's just wait and see."

Lori D'Angelo is the recipient of a grant from the Elizabeth George Foundation and an alumna of the Community of Writers. Her work has appeared in journals such as BULL, Moon City Review, and Salvation South. Her first book, The Monsters Are Here, was published by ELJ Editions in 2024. Originally from Pittsburgh, she earned her MFA from West Virginia University. She lives in central Virginia.

THE CHRISTMAS THE RAILROAD CAME

BRUCE WETTERAU

"That Christmas? Reckon I remember it right well."

"Tell us the story, Grandpa. Please," Sarah pleaded, her little girl eyes imploring him. With her hair tied in skinny pigtails, she was, at ten, the youngest of the three grand-children sitting on the worn, oval rug at the old man's feet. Alongside her a gangly lad of twelve, towheaded Grover, mischievously elbowed his twin brother, Calvin Jr. Calvin pushed him back hard.

A fire burned lazily in the stone fireplace before them, adding a yellow glow to the dim light cast by a gaslight chandelier suspended over the old man's living room. The smell of wood smoke mingled with the sharp, sweet scent of pine and the mouthwatering aroma of pies baking in the kitchen. Christmas cards lined the fringes of the big mirror above the fireplace, and if you looked closely you might see emblazoned on some the message, "Happy 1901! We lived to see the New Century." Red and white striped stockings stuffed with as yet unopened presents hung from the mantel below the mirror. And the old man's Christmas tree filled a far corner of the room. Gaily colored glass balls, a garland of popcorn strung on a thread, and a yellow star at the top decorated the tree.

Grandpa smiled faintly as he pretended to be reluctant. "Hain't I told you that'n afore?"

"Tell us again, please Grandpa!" Sarah cried out.

"Well, since y'all insist." He paused, thinking back. "I swear, it was a Christmas to beat all, an' I seen sixty-three of 'em, mind you.

"I was 'bout your age — twelve I reckon — that there Christmas. Eighteen hunnert an' fifty-two it was, an' Salem wasn't nothin' but a handful of houses an' such. Oh, we was the Roanoke County seat sure enough, an' we had a blacksmith shop, an' a silversmith shop, an' three hotels, an' two churches, an' even a little college then. But bein' up in the Blue Ridge Mountains like we was, we was a frontier town, two days ride west from the closest city, Lynchburg.

"So livin' was a little bit rougher than you kids got now, but me and Calvin, my little brother, we made do. Mostly things was quiet and peaceful. The Indian troubles was gone and Pa had him twenty acres cleared. We had pigs an' chickens an' he growed stuff too. Vegetables for Ma to put up and tobaky, mostly. Seemed like we was either workin' real hard at the chores or bored stiff watchin' the stuff grow. But covered wagons, trappers, and such was always passing through town on the road west, so we had some excitement. Gold rush was on then. We seen our share of them poor souls headin' west, their noggins all full of gettin' rich dreams. Leastwise that's what the preacher said.

"Anyhows, some years afore the Christmas I'm speakin' of, folks at Lynchburg got right determined that a railroad to Bristol City in Tennessee made too much sense. Said lots of money kin be made transportin' people and goods up here and beyond. Someday maybe even run east far as Richmond and west far as New Orleans. Like the railroad do nowadays.

"Mind you, railroads was a new thing back then and not cheap to build neither. I think the men wantin' 'em was called visionaries. Sometimes they was called dang fools too. But anyhow, the first leg of that Virginia Tennessee Railroad — that's what they called her back then — run right to Salem.

"They was adiggin' an' agradin' an' abuildin' an' such for years afore them rails finally got to Salem, so they was plenty of time for folks to get excited, or hateful, about it being finished. I reckon we had mostly the first kind, an' only a few 'tother.

"So the train was 'a comin'. Tracks was laid all the way from Lynchburg to Salem. They was a passel more work to do from Salem to Bristol, and money was runnin' tight. But trains was set to start regalar runs to Salem. So them visionaries — or fools, take yer pick — come up with the idea of makin' it a big celebration.

"It were a Wednesday, De-cember 15, nigh on Christmas, that they loaded up two trains in Lynchburg with them railroad company bigwigs, the Lynchburg artillery company an' rifle guards, an' all manner of local folks wantin' to ride a train an' celebrate somethin'. Warn't no trouble fillin' up both trains, I expect. An' as big a crowd I ever see'd in my young life was millin' about that railhead east of Salem town, waitin' for them trains.

"I remember they was late. It was cloudy that day and people was gettin' right impatient standin' out there in the cold and all. Calvin and me was plenty warm in our buckskin frocks and coonskin caps. Ya don't see them caps much anymores, but they was right warm.

"So we wasn't cold, but we sure was bored waitin'. We cured it by runnin' a good ways along the tracks 'till Ma yelled, 'Stop you rascals! Keep off them tracks or I'll tan your hides.' Ma was always promisin' to do that, but she never did. It was always Pa swingin' that switch.

"Anyhows, me and Calvin figgered it was our job to keep a lookout for that train, an' I reckon he was the first one ever to put his ear on the track to see if a train was acomin'. Mind you, Calvin was always the curious one, wantin' to know how things was jiggered. An' all by hisself he figgered out puttin' your ear on that iron track. Well, that day he done it about twenty times afore he heard the train. Rest of the time he complained plenty about how cold that iron was on his ear. Claimed it was frostbit.

"When Calvin did hear it finally about two o'clock, we run like the dickens to tell Pa. But soon as we got there, somebody yelled 'I see smoke.' So Calvin didn't get no thanks for his frostbit ear.

"Warn't a minute later that big ole engine came achuffin' an' ahuffin' an' ascreechin' to a stop afore the crowd, smoke ablowin' all over us and steam hissin' outa that engine like some monster snake about to bite yah."

Grandpa suddenly reached out and pretended to bite Calvin Jr. with his fingers. Little Calvin scrambled out of reach while the other two grandchildren giggled with delight. "Almost gotcha!" Grandpa shouted and laughed. Then he took up his story again.

"By then everbody was aclappin' and cheering their heads off. Pretty quick all them folks from Lynchburg started comin' off those fancy-lookin' passenger cars too. Me and Calvin, bein' smaller than all them grownups, did our best to keep from gettin' stepped on in all the jostlin', handshakin', an' backslapping.

"Pa made us stay with him and Ma to listen to the speeches, which far as Calvin and me was concerned was all high soundin' huffery. But we sure liked all the smoke and noise of the canon salutes and rifle salutes to celebrate the day.

"An' the barbecue too. They was roast pig, beef, an' chicken, all kinds o' put up preserves, cakes, cookies, pies galore, cider, an' beer. Calvin and me stuffed ourselfs. Then it bein' dark now and so much goin' on, Calvin whispers to me that we kin drift away casual like an' climb up on that big locomotive. See what she was like inside.

"So that's what we done. We know'd we wasn't supposed to be climbin' up there, and I worried plenty about bein' caught. Everthin' was still pretty hot inside that there engine cab, an' to me it smelt like we stuck our heads in a fireplace full of burnt wood. But ole Calvin he was in seventh heaven touching all them gauges an' levers an' such. It musta all got too much for him, 'cause he started afiddlin' with a lever comin' up outa the floor. 'Wonder what this does,' he says. Right quick I says don't mess with that Calvin! But he done it anyway, released that lever so's it snapped forward like.

"At first nothin' happened. Calvin and me just stared at each tother wide-eyed an' lookin' mighty scared. Then gradual like the train she started rollin' backwards. 'Calvin! What have you done?' I yelled at him."

"'Help me, Arty,' he says. 'It's stuck an' I cain't get her back.' An' I says to him, we gonna roll all the way back to Lynchburg ifn' you don't do somethin' quick."

"How far was that, Grandpa?" Sarah asked excitedly.

"A good two days or more walkin', for sure darlin'.

"So Calvin an' me was pushin' with all our might but that there lever didn't budge an inch. I'm thinking I ain't never seen Lynchburg but I'm sure gonna now!

"'Bout then felt like we was movin' along pretty good when all of a sudden we crashed into sumthin'. Knocked me an' Calvin to the floor an' banged our noggins good too.

"Right quick people came a runnin' an' we didn't get no chance to run, so we was caught red-handed. Everbody said we was lucky that the second train was parked behind us. They was some damage to the last passenger car when we rolled into the train, but people said that could be fixed easy.

"Pa took Calvin and me by the scruff of our necks an' brung us right up to that Mr. Donahue. He run the railroad an' I heard tell he about had a fit of apoplexy when he heard the crash. Pa said we was just kids an' we was right sorry for any damage we done. Calvin he said it was all his fault — he just wanted to see how it worked — so please don't stop the trains coming to Salem on account of him. Then Pa made me an' Calvin promise we'd never do nuthin' like that again. Seemed like that mellowed the man some, 'cause he even smiled a little.

"Didn't help us none with Ma and Pa though. They took us straight home so's we missed the fireworks. Ma said we was bad boys, an' so far she was concerned we wouldn't get no Christmas presents. Then Pa took us out to the woodshed for a tannin'. Warn't much though. Pa said real serious like, 'You're old enough, you shoulda know'd better.' But he was sorta laughin' when he said me and Calvin was gonna be famous for trying to wreck the railroad on the very first day it come to town.

"Next day Pa punished me and Calvin some more by makin' us stack a coupla cords of firewood he split. When we done that all neat and tidy, he said it bein' almost Christmas and all, we was outa the doghouse and we'd get our presents after all. Me and Calvin was mighty relieved, I tell you.

"That warn't the last of it though. That Sunday, the preacher give a special sermon about boys an' the trouble they get into 'cause of their curiosity. Calvin and me was mighty red faced an' slunk down in our pew, 'cause everbody was grinnin' and lookin' right at us.

"Come Christmas mornin' we was openin' our presents when Pa brought out two he had hid special. They was both toy locomotives carved outa' wood that the railroad had made particular for Calvin and me! Pa laughed an' said Mr. Donahue wanted us to play with them an' leave his real ones alone.

"I was pleased well enough that we was outa trouble for what we done, but ole Calvin, he loved that little wooden engine a powerful lot. I'm guessin' that's why I wound up takin' over Pa's farm an' ole Calvin, he worked twenty-odd years for the railroad. Best dang engineer they ever had."

Roanoker Bruce Wetterau is a freelance writer, novelist and nonfiction author who has written seventeen books. His Clay Cantrell Mystery series now has three titles in print and he is at work on a fourth installment.

His most recent book is a collection of short stories, What My Refrigerator Said to Me — Misadventures in the Digital Age. Among his nonfiction works are

The Presidential Medal of Freedom, Winners and Their Achievements, and Congressional Quarterly's Desk Reference on American Government.

UNTRADITIONAL BLUE RIDGE CHRISTMAS

DEBBIE SEAGLE

As always, Nana burst through the door with her arms in the air, let a little squeal, and embraced each of us as we stepped onto her porch. Snow was blanketing the mountains with blinding force and every member of our family arrived just in time to get snowed in for Christmas.

That was my favorite Christmas. My best memory in life. Our last big Christmas.

Appalachian snow added fascination to our family holiday that particular year. Once everyone was accounted for, we congregated on the front porch suspended in silence as snow drifted to earth and surrounded us with a hush of white. We marveled, as if we'd never seen such magic. I still feel it.

Silence, in our family, was as uncommon as tea without sugar, yet we huddled together with a sense of wonder... in peace... full of love. Silent. I remember inhaling the clean mountain air and watching the falling snow sparkle behind the porch light. We stood without words.

Can you feel it?

From the time Christmas was invented, our family embraced the joy of knowing that Christmas at Nana's house in the Southwest Virginia Highlands was everything we were about. No one missed Nana's Christmas dinner. Ever. It was tradition.

Christmas music, the sizzle of fried oyster dressing, and outbursts of laughter fill my memories. The boys relocated the nativity scene and turned on the football game. Sweet potatoes and marshmallows filled the air, mingling with the scent of cinnamon and cloves from simmering cider.

Year after year, Nana pulled the turkey, ham, corn pudding, and bubbling mac n cheese from the oven to make room for pumpkin pie, green bean casserole, and rolls. Christmas cookies and candies covered coffee tables. Everyone ate a piece of Nana's fruitcake, or pretended to.

We played the same board games, gobbled Nana's homemade peanut butter chocolate balls, and chased dogs around the house. Nana hugged everyone a third time, then stepped out to have a talk with Santa. At least that's what she told us. But I smelled smoke coming from her Canning Shed out back.

As tradition would have it, we rearranged name cards on the table — and arranged the NOEL blocks on the mantle to read LEON. In response, Nana set a place at the table for LEON and put her stuffed giraffe in the seat in front of Leon's plate. We were the only hillbillies with a Christmas giraffe.

After the blessing, Nana made sure we had our napkins on our laps. It was a thing. Gravy, butter, and jokes were passed around the long table, and everyone talked at once.

There was never a kid's table. Folding tables added to both ends of the dining table extended into the living room, covered in tablecloths with the theme of the year. That snowy year's theme was White Christmas.

Nana knew it was going to snow (she claimed it was forecast in her arthritis, but we all knew she had the weather channel). So, everyone was persuaded to wear white snowball hats and sit at the table with a huge white bib and fake white eyebrows. Traditional Christmases were not your Hallmark traditional scene in our family. That was the tradition.

One year, the theme was baby Jesus. Another year it was Elf (of course mounds of candy canes lined the table and a large bowl of spaghetti with maple syrup was on the menu). There was a silver bells candlelight-themed Christmas, complete with sparklers that set off the fire alarm. Years past showcased Snowmen, Reindeer, Santa, and Griswold family Christmas.

The Griswold Christmas-light extravaganza blew a fuse, true to the theme. Nana's huge tree toppled over, and I still believe she orchestrated that. A burned turkey complemented the always burned rolls.

Everyone agreed that they had grown to expect and appreciate burned bread with meals Nana cooked. It was her trademark. The grandchildren joked that the first time they had rolls somewhere else, they assumed the bread was undercooked (without the dark buttered

crust). We were raised on crunchy blackened ham biscuits.

The Santa year — 12 large Santas dominated the table.
Most of the food was shaped like Santa Clause. The
cookies and Jello mold — obviously Santa shaped. But
she "dressed" the turkey like Santa and the vegetable
tray silhouetted Santa.

Nana was the original charcuterie board artist.

After dinner, the legendary ball of surprises was passed
around the circle. When the Christmas music stopped,
the person holding the ball unwrapped the next gift
layer. We were never surprised to find butt wipes, a
bag of candy, a DVD, a Grinch ski hat, gift cards, ski
gloves, movie tickets, goat soap, or a P. Diddy or New
Kids on the Block CD. The center of Nana's "jingle ball,"
the last surprise, was always something she cherished
and wanted someone in the family to have.

Nana generously distributed (too many) gifts that took
her all year to assemble for her three daughters
and our families. Everyone received a stocking filled
with socks, hand-made mittens, chapstick, flashlights,
whoopie cushions, and toilet paper with someone's face
printed on it. There were harmonicas, juggling balls,
rubber chicken support animals, and calendars with
everyone's birthday filled in.

One year, Nana added condoms, pooping candy dis-
pensers, and tampons. She loved watching her grandchildren exchange glances. No one commented on the
embarrassing and inappropriate stocking-stuffers. We
respected her and cherished Nana's eccentric sense of
humor, for the most part. She'd watch us, smiling sweet-
ly, and oh so innocently.

That Christmas when everyone was snowed in on top
of the mountain was the year everyone cried laughing -

watching old VCR recordings of our childhood awkwardness. Quotes from those videos added to family lore and years of ribbing.

We watched ourselves (as naked babies) running through the sprinkler, skateboarding recklessly, and blowing out candles, all while sporting outdated hairstyles and hideous clothing. That was a hit with our children, and should have made them question their style choices. But it didn't.

A few years back, her grandchildren were jumping on the bed, and it was all fun and games until Nana joined in. There were stitches. Naturally, Nana led a caroling group through the corridors of the hospital, until she got 16 of us kicked out. Only Nana could inject an emergency room with singing, riotous behavior, and festivity.

Snow forts and snowball fights were usually Nana's idea. Years without snow, Nana was ready with fake snowballs and Nerf guns. Back then though, there was usually snow.

Nana customarily decorated every inch of the house. It never failed: the motion-detected snowman would sing bathroom songs to anyone who sat on the toilet. Other areas of her house featured a talking Christmas tree, and a singing fish on the wall (donning a Santa hat). It all added to the annoyingly delightful mayhem.

Her house was proudly adorned in Family. Cut-out handprints (of all of us) were hung on her tree. Framed photos of us in reindeer ears, matching PJs, and elf costumes decorated her shelves and end tables.

Every Christmas was coated in sugar, laughter, and lore. The joy of family was everything to Nana, and Christmas was when she could count on her family to show up.

Her invitations to family picnics were randomly attended. Thanksgiving was usually stolen by our in-laws.

Groundhog Day — she always had a party we didn't attend. But everyone called Nana with a creative excuse for not celebrating Punxsutawney Phil on February 2nd.

Christmas, that was Nana's. Having her family together for whirlwind activity made her glow. It made her life meaningful and worthwhile. For decades, Nana delighted in gathering her family. Until COVID.

The mandates to stay home uprooted our family tradition and proved just how easy it was to control a population with propaganda and fear. Nana spent Christmas Eve and Christmas Day alone that year.

We called her. We called her the following few years too. She pretended to be cheerful, but her voice sounded shaky and weak.

The past few years, there were babies born, family flu, sudden fear of snow, and work obligations that sequestered some of us in different parts of the country. Me, I died last year; and sadly, Nana's blue eyes haven't twinkled as brightly since. I was her favorite. She told me so.

Once a tradition is broken, all the little pieces seem to scatter. It can't be repaired. My children and one of my sisters visit her occasionally. I watch over her, but she doesn't recognize me. She talks to me. But then, she talks to the washing machine when it gets off-balance.

My disjointed family won't realize, until they watch the videos again, how much they miss our big family gatherings, how much they long for the enchantment of Nana's house and the loving energy around her table. Someday each of them will recall their favorite memory ... the beauty of nature and simplicity ... that rare feeling of unconditional love ... silliness ... and the warmth of a close-knit Appalachian family.

If I could, I'd get the family together for another Christmas at Nana's, just to see her face light up again. But that's not going to happen. This is her last Christmas, and she will spend it alone again looking out into her snow-dusted mountains in hopes of a miracle. Longing for family.

There's nothing traditional about that.

Debbie Seagle lives in the Blue Ridge Mountains of Virginia. She's a #1 bestselling, award-winning author/screenwriter, and former newspaper columnist. Her book Coffee Cups & Wine Glassesis being made into a movie. The film is inspired by true events based on her memoir, which is based on some bad decisions that turned into hilarious material (if you're not Debbie).
Her photography, newspaper and magazine articles have been published worldwide. She loves her family, friends, writing, kayaking, skiing, hiking, her maker, her country, and her truck. Her background as an airshow director, Top Secret technical writer, mother of three sons, and MiMi inspires her writing.

CRIMSON IN BLUE WILLOW

MARJORIE GOWDY

In two days, at winter solstice, family and friends will gather in the log-beamed dining room of Molly Spencer's sprawling house on The 100-Acre Farm. Her ex, loquacious Alban Alonzo Joyce III, will march in with cases of Bordeaux. If this is a year when they've been friendly with each other, the country lawyer might also tote a gallon of oysters. Buddy Lopez, local deputy and prize baker of fruit pies, will enter by Molly's kitchen door while Frederick and Charlie, her beloved neighbors, will roar through the old, wide wild cherry entrance out front, arms full of lavender and hot house greens from their farm. Her children, the ever-observant Fawn, and Wrenn with his beautiful wife and bundle of children, will arrive with cakes, breads, and butter-rich mashed potatoes.

Always a lively gathering in the 150-year-old farmhouse, these loyal companions of Molly don't see what she sees in herself: the supposedly confident editor of a rural online newspaper with a complete lack of skill in the kitchen. (Correction: they know she can't cook more than the most basic of meals, but except for Alban's jests, these loved ones look right past that.)

They also can't see what else Molly sees: three ephemeral figures standing just outside her filigree windows, there to aid her at every turn. Her invisible friends have worked with Molly over the years to solve problems ranging from the mundane (where did I leave that lopper?) to the serious, once-threatening series of murders in this quiet valley below the Blue Ridge Mountains.

Tied by blood and separated only by dimension, the trio and Molly are inseparable companions whose relationship is unknown to the people who in 48 hours will mill in good cheer around Molly's table.

Today, two days before solstice, China Alice, Tankita, and Jay approach Molly, her head down, weathered gloves in tussled silver-sandy hair. "I just give up," Molly says. "The only thing I ever serve at solstice dinner is a burned casserole. Or sometimes half-dried cranberries."

Jay, the son whom Molly and Alban lost to a damned disease years before, winks, transparent eyes framed by his trademark fringe of blond hair. "I think this year we can help you."

*

Each year as dogwood berries redden and as American bittersweet fruit entices wintering mockingbirds, Molly feels an urge to get out her baking pans. In this narrow valley, winter announces itself in late November each year with a sharp "boom" as west winds whip over the nearby plateau and bump hard into the Blue Ridge. Molly heard the boom last night. This morning in the grey sift of sunlight, the wind howls. It is time to cook. "Thank God for my invisible friends," she says.

That connection to companions whom only she can see has always been a force in Molly's long life. Such mystic camaraderie started when Molly turned four and her grandfather, a city banker reared on No Business Mountain and a believer in the unseen, introduced her to Miss Elsie. Molly kept Miss Elsie in a paper bag. As a young woman, Molly was visited by characters including a plump figure in a house rumored to have been built atop graves of Revolutionary War soldiers. The apparition didn't say much but was a comfort in those winsome days.

Now, as her hair looks like remains of dunes on a wind-swept beach, Molly often has callers — not just the neighbors — to The 100-acre farm. The visits began several springs back when two figures outside her studio warned of pending danger. Editor of a rural online newspaper, Molly disclosed her new invisible friends to no one. Together, they solved a mystery and have since worked on several more.

"You need us," the transparent yet stern figure of China Alice first said to Molly as another, lithe young woman, Tankita, nodded and gestured. "Come over here and know us." Those first words, spoken yet not, evolved into an almost sacred, secret dialog between intimates. After their first adventure, China Alice and Tankita brought along a third, treasured guest, Jay. Jay of her saddest dreams. He of the twinkling eyes and cotton candy hair.

China Alice and Tankita sometimes brought Molly a trinket: old lace, the beak of an ancient hawk, and, as autumn left, dogwood berries. The berries Molly shared with hungry cardinals; the trinkets she lined up along the chestnut mantle in her great room.

Wee Jay has yet to bring her anything, but Molly's memories stir of her little boy in a grocery cart, with strangers commenting too loudly on his large head and tiny body. The cruel passersby were never immersed in Jay's enchantment, a magic shared only with his family and closest friends. Those fortunate to be introduced knew a boy buying extra time while spreading infectious joy and mischief. During their few short winter holidays together, Molly and Jay took home from the store cranberries, which together they stirred into sweet dough to bake a rich, bread-like pastry. Jay called it his "Red Cake." Molly found the color more like a crimson quickening every time she looked at Jay.

The corporeal body of China Alice is buried at the Head of the River Church up on the plateau. There, in the 1800s, the stout woman raised three children, including Molly's great-grandmother Oakey, who became a legendary country cook. Each summer, at their church's "Association," Oakey took pots of fatback beans, red eye gravy, sugar-cured ham, soda biscuits, and her specialty, fried apple pies. The stark black dresses of churchwomen faded into a background of steaming soups, cherry-brimmed desserts, and chopped lettuce salads. Oakey's talent in the kitchen was passed down the generations — although it appeared to have skipped by Molly.

Born in the early 1700s, Tankita learned to cook from her Mahala and aunts. The Tutelo tribe of the mountains near Big Lick were a peaceful lot who raised corn and potatoes and thrived on the flora and fauna of this valley fed by a rocky stream and fresh springs. Tankita loved nothing more as a child than making a bowl of corn and tomatoes for her father, a kind, wise man. Later, before their lives were taken by escaped prisoners, Tankita would make succotash for her Scots lover. Both rest now in the meadow where they were killed, covered by leaves of poplar and oak. Their son was reared by China Alice's grandparents.

And the body of little Jay is nestled in a cocoon of tears in the old German cemetery on The 100-Acre Farm.

Molly shivers in her warm studio whenever the trio of invisible friends approaches, appearing slowly out of the mountain. China Alice with a bun pulled firmly behind her head, Tankita in leather and leaves, and Jay with feathery yellow hair. They appear randomly but seem to prefer late autumn and the first warm days of spring. The three also cajole Molly outside to dance, regardless of weather, at winter and summer solstice. Known widely as a klutz, Molly finds her sea legs as she dances with her three transparent mates.

Knowing that others' original recipes will shine at this winter's upcoming feast, Molly has tried but failed to make something fresh and delicious. Too-flat cookies, odd-tasting stews, even the honey pecans had a funny look. Perhaps her invisible friends could share a recipe or two. She sits on the cold stone steps and waits for them.

"Over there, by the old mill," says China Alice, approaching through the early morning mist. "I know it's a cold wind blowing, but the lower rocks fell down in last week's flood. Something shiny is sticking out. We will lead you."

"Mama," the gossamer voice says, "this is my gift. Just follow us." Jay skips down the frosted pathway. "We have an idea for solstice dinner."

Tankita waits as the thin boy, his Mama, and China Alice cross the river and clamber up to the mill's only remaining wall. Stacked stones twice Molly's height lead up to the old homestead where river-scattered rocks make an uneasy walk down to a roaring run. While Molly can see the wall right through the three figures, she also sees what makes the three ephemeral comrades timeless: a bright plaid shawl around the shoulders of China Alice, a tattoo of berry dye on Tankita's legs and arms, and Jay's signature Top Gun jacket. The boy leans into the fallen rocks. "Look here, Mama. These fell out when the wind went boom."

Jay pulls a tightly sealed tin out of a hole in the rocks. Beside it are shards of Blue Willow ware from long ago. "I found these treasures for you. Make something for Daddy and your friends out of this. We're sure you can do it."

Molly picks up the rusted tin container and gingerly opens it. A cloud of yellowed flour floats out. Tankita places a basket of dogwood berries at her feet. "I can't use this old grain and these cold, wild berries." Molly looks at her friends. "Or can I?"

"You can make my Red Cake," says Jay. "Maybe the people can't eat it, but they'll remember how we used to bring them loaves every winter."

"Then you can give the cake to the birds," says China Alice, long a fan of the phoebes, sparrows and redbirds who nestle in laurels against the mountain. China Alice and Tankita often leave a trail of dogwood berries and bittersweet fruit for mockingbirds.

Jay, Tankita, and China Alice disappear into the ice-dappled rocks of the mill. Molly gathers the berries, flour tin, and pieces of Blue Willow. The next day, while a fire crackles below the mantlepiece lined with trinkets from her invisible companions, Molly stirs up Jay's Red Cake. As it bakes, she repairs the Blue Willow bowl. By morning, a crimson-stained loaf of buttery bread sits cooling in her window. Solstice arrives this evening.

Day setting a cool rose over the mountains, Molly's family and neighbors gather around the groaning walnut table. "Glad I brought oysters this year," Alban jostles, nodding to the table full of children and friends. "Otherwise, we'd starve." Walnut planks heave with cherry pies, sugar cookies, herb-scented casseroles, and rich wines.

Molly, not one for emotion, feels her face flush from the warmth of the fire and candlelight as a perfect Red Cake takes center stage in the Blue Willow bowl. No one touches the loaf. They whisper to each other that Molly seems to see the Red Cake as a kind of talisman and suspect she is saving it for another time. But they all share oohs and ahhs at the crimson glow of the warm berry-filled cake. "Why, Mama," Fawn laughs, "do you always say you can't cook?"

Jay, China Alice, and Tankita peer through the filigree windows as the feast proceeds. Twinkles in her boy's eyes mimic the stars' tribute to the turning of the season. Soon, Molly steps outside in the teasing wind to dance beneath the sky.

Nearby, birds in winter's apparel wait in bare branches for tomorrow's feast on Red Cake in the Blue Willow bowl.

Marjorie Gowdy, a retired museum director and grants writer, writes and paints on a farm in the Blue Ridge Mountains of Virginia. Author of three poetry chapbooks, her latest is Pillow Fight, published in 2024. While working on a book of poems, Confessions from the Bottomland, she is also beginning to write fiction, including short stories as well as a novel of historical fantasy.

CHALKING UP OLD CHRISTMAS

BILL KOVARIK

A chill in the autumn air, a thrill at the back of your neck, a thumping in th' heart, and that squeaking terror in your strangled scream .... Sure, most people think that's what happens when you bump up against the supernatural. But it ain't so.

I know this 'cause I was born on Old Christmas Day — January 6 — which is celebrated in mountain lore as the day of healing and protection.

Two ways, now, that you can get protection. One is by burying the guts of a black chicken under the hearth to guard against fire and lightning. Or, if you're a tad less superstitious, you can chalk the door. It's easy. You just mark the year, with the three wise men in the middle.

So, the year was 1939, and a'course the wise men were Caspar, Melchior and Balthazar, so I chalked the door like this: 19+C+M+B+39.

The protection doesn't come from the rituals themselves. It comes when you realize the duty we all owe to the protective spirits, the guardian angels — you know, your ancestors who gather 'round the hearth.

Elwyna used to tell us that she didn't believe in such-like, but they were there all the same. I used to wonder about that.

Elwyna was my mom's great aunt who promised to take care of us. She was a toothless old widder-woman who lived all her life back up the next holler. She raised baccy for her corncob pipe and batched up corn squeezins now and then. "Drink a few shots and you are set, you dancin' fool," Elwyna would say. "Drink down a whole pint an' your woman will go home with another man."

Elwyna's garden grew the biggest turnips and pumpkins you've ever seen, which was on account of plantin' by the signs. But her true gift was healing, because she, too, was born on January 6.

On my sixteenth birthday in 1939, I chalked the door, and then took a notion to bag a deer, what with the corn meal running low and the lard bucket not looking like it would make it to next week, much less Fat Tuesday.

Cousin Ferdy lived in the holler, so I fetched her up, and told her to grab her rifle, for to be my second shot. If'n you don't know about hunting deer, it's handy to have a second rifle because the deer can sense the first shot coming and take a leap. The second shot goes high, up front.

We wandered off into the clouds grazing the mountain, and we crept through the rhododendron forest towards the spring above Elwyna's garden, where the deer love to linger in the late afternoon. Elwyna doesn't like us hunting there. It disturbs the peace of the place, she says.

But we were hungry and not thinking very clearly.

Ferdy an' I came across a young buck in the fog, and I drew a bead but then I stopped. "Don't …" I whispered, but the buck jumped and Ferdy fired, and in a second we had turned a thing of beauty into a hunk of raw meat.

So Elwyna comes running up to the sound of the shot madder'n all hell, saying we'd runed it, just runed it. But then the deer staggered to its feet and wandered down the holler to her front porch.

I was feeling sorrowful and stupid. "Damn, Ferdy, what in hell's wrong with us?" I whispered.

Then Elwyna sat down with the deer on her porch, cradling its head, muttering some old Scottish prayers. I knew she was a powerful healer, and she could fix the mistake we made.

And at first, I thought she did fix it. The deer stood up gracefully and walked away in the silver moonlight. Watching that, I felt a powerful blend of color, and warmth, and freedom of spirit, like the Seann Triubhas dance at a summer Highland festival. It almost seemed as if the gates of heaven opened for that deer, and then slammed shut for us.

"How did you do that, Elwyna?" I asked.

"Do what?"

"Heal that deer and make it walk away," I explained.

"Don't be crazy," she said. "Here's your deer."

She was right. The carcass was right there. She was cradling it on the porch.

"Better clean it before you walk home, or it'll go rancid," she said, with a small, sniffling smile.

"How is that possible?" I asked. "We just saw the deer walk off down the trail."

Ferdy nodded. "I saw it too," she said.

Elwyna drew a deep breath and looked us over with a kind of love but also a sadness, and her voice took on a strange starry quality: deep, cold, and distant.

"You saw the best part of that deer, walking the same trail that you will walk someday," the deep sad voice said.

"And don't look so proud of yourselves, knowing what you know now. Cause the days are coming when you will be tested, and you are going to have to remember that this world doesn't just bump up against the next one by accident. This world is the pale shadow, the wisp of fog, the breeze in the moonlight. That other world you saw — that's the real one. And now you're going to ache for it."

She pulled a wisp of hair back behind her pointed ear and shook her head at us.

"Most people ain't given to know ... all that. They never learn that the end of this life is not the end of life itself. And that's for a reason. Most people would take that knowledge and use it recklessly, without care or forethought.

"But you, nephew, born on Old Christmas day, and you, Ferdy, will have to carry that ache the rest of what is going to be two very long lives."

She was right.

I carried the ache through Tunisia, and Sicily, and Normandy in the 1940s, along with the stretchers that I lifted in and out of surgery. I carried it through medical school in Virginia in the 1950s, and through the lives and deaths of two wives, five children and a few unlucky grandchildren in the decades that followed. Cousin Ferdy too, not long ago.

I watched as each one of them wandered down that path, in that moonlight, with that damned old deer. And every time, I prayed to God, trying to give the thanks I should have given ol' Elwyna that January 6 back when my world was still young.

I can still feel that breeze, muffled in the cold fog of a late mountain evening.

In fact, it's getting closer.

Bill Kovarik is a writer and college professor who teaches journalism, media law and history at Radford University in Virginia.

On Catawba Road: A Curious Encounter

Richard Raymond III

The odd thing about it, it was nowhere near Christmas Eve, when old-time folks would gather about the fire, sip hot toddies and tell ghost stories to chill the blood. In simple fact, it was about sundown on a raw November day. Earlier, there had been a spat of rain go through, and the blacktop road was still glistening wet. I was on my way back to Roanoke from a Masonic lodge meeting in New Castle for initiation of a candidate, the most ordinary thing imaginable.

Not far ahead loomed the great dark bulk of Catawba Mountain, a long, winding road to the summit, then a snake-hipped dance down the other side to the bottoms of Mason Creek. This road doesn't get a lot of traffic, and on a gloomy afternoon in 1996 the sight of a lone figure trudging along the highway was enough to make me pause. I eased off on the gas and flicked my lights.

Pedestrians are supposed to walk on the left side, facing traffic, but this was a girl, hardly more than a teen-ager, I thought, who moved steadily along, just on the right shoulder. Until I pulled up alongside her, she never so much as looked around.

Hitting the window-down button, I called across, "Hi there, miss, are you all right? Out here all by your lonesome, it's getting dark, not a good time to be on the road. Very dangerous, cars come by here fast, not see you. Could I give you a lift?" She stopped, looked in at me.

In the back-shine of my headlights, I gave her closer scrutiny. She was not tall, but showed an excellent figure, pale complexion, with long, unbound chestnut tresses falling down her back. Her face — I shall never forget it — an almost ethereal beauty, blue eyes, long lashes, short straight nose, slightly dusted with freckles, full lips, curved in a mysterious smile. She was dressed far too lightly for this weather — a sky-blue blouse and skirt, no coat, not even a sweater, long stockings and fancy pumps on her feet. What could have possessed her to come out like this? She must have been nearly freezing.

For a moment she gazed at me, then spoke, her voice a sweet melody. "I'm going home, my mama must be very worried that I haven't gotten home. And it's such a long way to walk."

I was stunned. The houses on this road are few and far between, and for this slip of a girl to be going it on foot was beyond folly, it was madness. "Miss," I asked, "where is your home? Is it up ahead? I'd be glad to take you there. This is much too dangerous for you."

Again, that mystic smile. "Oh, I live on Bradshaw Road, over toward Salem. It won't take me long."

That floored me. "But miss, that's nearly seven miles over the mountain, you can't be meaning to walk! Please, please get in the car, I promise I'll take you right home." I leaned over and opened the passenger-side door. For one breathless moment she paused, then gracefully slid in, stretching her feet to the floorboard. "Thank you so much," she murmured, "I really was getting tired."

"Buckle up," I said, as she pulled the door shut. "Driver's rule, gotta buckle up." She looked at me in astonishment, her glorious blue eyes wide. A man could get lost in them.

"Buckle up? What on earth is that?"

For one long moment I stared back. Was she serious? Then, not to risk more time stopped on the highway's edge, I reached over, pulled the seat-belt strap around her and snapped it into the catch.

"Okay, now we can go." Another minute, we were flying. "Well, miss, and what's your name? Mine's Ross. Short for Rossiter, which I've never liked much." I threw a glance over at her, where she sat quietly, unmoving as a statue, staring out at the cone of headlights cutting through the gathering night.

"My name? Oh. Yes. Laurie. Laurie Wexford. I've never seen such a beautiful car. What's it called?"

Again, I was startled at her seeming lack of knowledge. The "H" for Honda was plain enough on the steering wheel, but she took no apparent notice of it. And this four-year-old Civic was anything but beautiful — if anything, this model was a utility infielder. Egads! I thought: this little gal is easily impressed.

I decided to probe a bit, without trying to be too nosy. "Er, Miss Laurie, how come you were so far out, with no way home? How'd you get there, anyway?"

"Oh, I came with a friend. He had a car. But then I had to get home, so I walked." My fake solicitude rolled off her like raindrops off a fresh wax job. She leaned her lovely head back against the pop-up headrest. This gal was nothing but mysterious, and the quicker I got her where she was going, the better I'd like it. By now, we were making knots up Catawba Mountain, the summit not far ahead.

All of a sudden, she sat up and cried, "Oh! Oh! We've got to stop! I've got to get out!" She fumbled at the seat-belt catch, not knowing how to get free. "Please, please!" she sobbed, "Please let me go, I've got to go home. Stop the car!"

Right at the peak of the pass on Catawba, there's a big old log cabin, been there for years. It's been a restaurant, a tourist lodge, several other things, at the moment was between owners, and every window was dark. I was flabbergasted by her sudden outburst, but most unwilling to have her leave, so pulling into the small parking space at the crest, I stopped the car and turned to her, saying, "What can be the matter? We're almost back to your home now! You can't get out and walk again, that's crazy!"

But she was weeping, crying, "No! No! Let me out, let me out! Spencer, I love you!" Somehow she managed to hit the seat-belt release, and quickly threw the door open. In a flash she had jumped out of the car, slammed the door and was running down the road.

Now get this. The present Virginia 311 highway from Salem is a huge improvement over the old road, which started right at the top, then zig-zagged down the hillside in a series of sharp switchbacks. I'd been down it once, in daylight, out of curiosity, which was quite enough for me. To drive down that abandoned road at night was not a rational choice. But the girl was running, running; in the light of my headlamps, I saw her turn and fly down that crooked blacktop to hell. Before I could have unstrapped myself, she was out of sight.

For perhaps five full minutes I sat there, almost paralyzed with shock. By now it was full black dark, and nothing but an owl could have navigated that road safely. Was I responsible for her? I had to assume that somewhere along the trail, she'd miss a turn and fall to her death.

As I slowly unbelted and stepped out of my car, a pair of headlights from the Salem side were swiftly approaching. I stood in the full glare as the car came up to the turn, then pulled to a stop with a crunch of tires on gravel. It was a county sheriff's cruiser. The driver rolled down his window and called, "You all right, there, mister? What gives?"

"I don't know," I answered, still full of doubt. "Can you come over here? I need to talk."

"Hold on," he said, and in a moment his spotlight speared me, searching back and forth to shine into my car and freeze me like a whitetail buck. I could hear him send a message back to the station, giving his location and apparent situation. Then, with a quick practiced movement, the deputy opened his door and ordered me to turn around and put my hands on the hood of my car. You can be sure I did exactly that, and did not move while he came up behind and patted me down. "Well, buddy, you're clean, but this is not the time and place for a rest stop. What say?"

"Officer, if I tell you the truth, will you not put the cuffs on me or call for backup? I'm clean, cold sober, and I think kind of scared." Then, without mincing words, I told him the story, while he stood, his face a study of police business. He was a big brawny kind of guy, and I'd no more have tried to bluff or snow him than I'd have kicked a grizzly bear in the butt.

Finally, with a serious expression, he said, "Describe the girl."

I did so, in as much detail as I could remember. "You say, she actually got in the car with you? Amazing. She's never done that before. Let me have a look inside." He produced a big five-cell flashlight, and I opened the passenger-side door, while he shined the light around. "Hmm," said he, pointing to the headrest. "Look there." The fabric, never too clean, was now stained with blood. In the crimson patch gleamed a single strand of rich chestnut hair.

"What!" I yelled, "She wasn't hurt when she got in, and I never touched her!" I was in a sweat, thinking that I'd be blamed for her injury.

"Son," said the deputy, gently, "that little lady was not what she seemed. Way back in nineteen and twenty-three, she was killed by her boyfriend, not far from here. Beat her head in and chucked her body into the Murder Hole. And you're not the first who's seen her, walking home along the road. She's a local legend. But you're the first I've known to give her a ride. She must have liked you.

"Yes, it was Laurie Wexford, pretty little girl from Mason's Cove. Her boyfriend died in Richmond Prison some ten years ago, about eighty-five years old. Name of Spencer Henry. Half-crazy with guilt, he was, at the end. If I were you, I'd just go home and have a drink, maybe make up a good story to tell your friends, come Christmas." With a smile and wave, he got back in his cruiser and drove away.

Next day I spent an hour cleaning the headrest. The hair, in a small white envelope, stays in my keepsake book.

Veteran author Richard Raymond III of Roanoke is a graduate of the U.S. Naval Academy, a retired engineer, and a member of the Virginia Writers Club. He has written a collection of short stories, Tales of the Fox; a book of Civil War poetry, Blue and Gray Ballads; and his newest collection, My Life With Holmes: The Further Reminiscences of John H. Watson, M.D.

FROSTBITE

KATHIE DICKENSON

December 25, 1931

Dear Jack,

Well, it was Christmas today. Jenny was all bright-eyed when she woke up and saw the tree. I asked Papa to look for a good one while he was out on his store rounds, and he brought it home on his truck last night. It is little, but Jack the smell fills up the house. I can't get enough of it. Mammyjane of course hasn't stopped talking about "that stinking cedar." If it makes me happy she don't want it. I guess Papa will take it out tomorrow. First light this morning tho he went out and shot down a bunch of mistletoe and we stuck it around in the branches and made it so pretty.

After Jenny was up, we went out and gathered pinecones and Papa held her up so she could put them in the tree. He bought her a little red sweater and told her it was from Santa. When he put it on her she hugged her arms around it and kept it on all day. When it came time for bed she was sitting in her little rocker by the front door like she does every night and said no, let me stay up till Daddy comes home so I can show him my sweater. My heart hurt.

When you picked me up and set us on that train, I kicked you. I would have hit you and bit you too if I could have reached but Jenny was in my arms. When you turned around and disappeared in the crowd, I felt like you were being swallowed up by the world.

I hope you have a warm coat to wear and keep your head covered when you are outside cutting lumber. You said Michigan winter would be too hard for us but if I was there I could knit you a hat and me and Jenny mittens. Don't get sick Jack.

It is winter in Virginia too. Christmas day was cold and clear and still, but by late afternoon it was clouding up and it feels like we might have snow tomorrow. Soon tho it will be spring and the baby will be born. If it's a boy, we'll name him Jack and maybe too if it's a girl. You will come home and get us then won't you. Mammyjane says she can't wait for you to get us out of her house but when she's feeling the meanest she'll say you know he's never coming for you. I want to bite her then.

Baskets of love,

Lena

xxoo

P.S. Why why why Jack don't you write back?

Kathie Dickenson has been a professional editor and writer for more than 30 years. Her freelance articles have appeared in magazines including Valley Business Front, Carilion Living, Roanoke Business, and Family Circle. Her short fiction and poems have appeared in the art and literary magazine Artemis and in alcalines, journal of the Assembly on the Literature and Culture of Appalachia. Kathie retired from Radford University, where she served in the Office of University Relations as senior writer and managing editor of the university's flagship magazine, and in the College of Education and Human Development as field experience coordinator.

A Six-Act Thanksgiving - 1972

Mark Fryburg

A roasted turkey, still steaming, sat at the top of the kitchen trash can, basted with cigarette ash. The room smelled like turkey meat, tobacco smoke, and beer. I had just arrived with my girlfriend, Helen Campbell, for my first Thanksgiving dinner with her family. Helen's mother, Louise, had apparently staged the carcass for high visibility. As we walked past it, brown bottle fragments crunched underfoot.

Helen's younger brother stood against the far wall, combing fingers through shoulder length red hair, a vacant gaze on his gaunt face.

Louise sat centerstage at a table set for five, wearing a ruffled cooking smock decorated with pumpkin silhouettes and a few grease smears. This tiny woman with messy brown hair stared at a half-spent Camel hanging between her fingertips, then back at the bird. Her free hand tightly squeezed the table's edge. At age 40, Louise's face displayed vertical cheek lines of hard, angry living. "Come on in," she muttered, not looking at us.

Helen and I had visited Louise at the Salem, Virginia, home several times before. Tonight she had warned me to expect high drama. Even then, I was startled, and a little frightened. Helen, aged 20 and an A-student, not quite as short as her mother, seemed calm and unsurprised, even prepared.

Our entry commenced Act II of the Campbell Family Holiday Play. The turkey's descent had signaled completion of Act I. It featured Louise's husband Roy (Big Roy), a shopworn 40-something I'd met but once. He had minutes ago left home in a rage, "shitfaced drunk ... pissing and moaning about his usual awful treatment by me and everybody else," Louise reported. "The bastard raised up his beer like he was gonna hit me, but he smashed it on the floor!" A door-slamming exit from the kitchen stage followed.

"Oh, wow," I said. I was 22, from a stable home environment where this portrayal just couldn't happen. I naively pointed to the garbage. "Louise, I am so sorry, but why the turkey thing?"

"What the hell do you think?" Louise screeched.

Helen shrugged. I retreated from the conversation, certain only that the remaining guests had an invitation to share her mother's misery, if not her sense of victimization.

Louise's dull blue eyes flashed with anger. "Well, at least it ain't as bad as last Christmas when Roy trashed the whole goddamn place!" She took a deep draw on a Budweiser, then her cigarette. "Of course, he could still come back and bust up everything tonight." She aimed a blank look at the corner.

"He's coming back?" I blurted, wide eyed.

"He won't be back," Helen said confidently. The tone indicated she'd seen this act before.

Other than that, Helen hadn't predicted specific performances. On the drive over, she had explained that "melodrama is my family's holiday tradition, sorta like how the It's a Wonderful Life movie is for others."

Her sibling, Little Roy, a slight boy of 12, had a blue-eyed, pale, pimple-free face destined for a mug shot in three years. He sullenly turned on his heels, a wordless surrender to his bedroom, to run some heavy Eric Clapton guitar on an 8-track stereo.

"Well, I guess I'll clean up," Helen said with an air of resignation, tying back her long dark brown hair out of the mess. She swept the glass shards. The counter, looking like an archeological dig, came next.

Attempting some holiday cheer, and an escape route, I proposed, "Why don't I take everyone out to Denny's?" Louise had once mentioned how much she savored a Denny's Steak and Baked Potato Special, followed by a big slice of pecan pie.

"I ain't hungry, Bill!" Louise shot back, looking like a rattler ready to strike.

Helen gave me the "Don't take this any further" look as Louise moved to martyr character, a soliloquy of injustices she suffered, but beginning with good times: "Y'all see, I fell for a handsome, blue eyed, redhead G.I. during the Korean War." The hopeful early years of new home and small children, Big Roy's bankruptcy as a service station owner, and his "wasted life as a worthless alcoholic" followed. Louise now had to do "everything myself" to keep the household together. She proclaimed with conviction that only her dedication to family kept her in the "sacred bonds of wedlock."

Helen rolled her eyes at me. Rather than commenting, she opened Act III with "Let's watch some TV!" She hollered it again towards Little Roy's sanctuary.

He shot out of the hall to the living room's black and white set. The bang of pro wrestlers hitting the mat replaced complaints from the kitchen. Helen and I followed, sinking into a well-stained sofa, holding hands. Louise joined us to quietly fume — and smoke — in a velour barrel chair. Little Roy's shouts of "Hit him. Slam him!" provided his sole remarks. My eyes turned to Helen's pretty heart-shaped face. She had a straight nose like her mom, inexplicable dark brown eyes that I loved and a deep half-inch scar above her left eyebrow, a mark she refused to discuss.

I thought, It's a shame Big Roy's missing the TV. I recalled my single encounter with this tall mechanic. He professed a love for pro wrestling. He spoke of "blowing ten bucks of precious beer money" to watch the sport live at the Starland Arena. I had attempted to convince him that it was just another staged melodrama.

"You can't tell me that's fake!" he argued, deep lines in his ruddy forehead rising. "Them boys are getting hurt. Just look at the blood!" Big Roy stayed sober for that part of the exchange. I suspected he also stayed clean at his current job as part-time mechanic at Franklin Road Ford. After rapidly downing several "Buds," Roy volunteered that he would have managed a great career, perhaps owning another gas station, maybe a restaurant, "If Louise hadn't always gotten in my way." (Helen later told me that Louise's wages as a registered nurse supplied most of the household income and supplemented Helen's Virginia Tech scholarship.)

The doorbell interrupted the TV audience's roar, signaling Act IV: The Neighborhood Nurse.

Enter next door neighbor Rhonda.

"Louise, you gotta come over right now. My Ricky musta ate somethin' really bad this time!"

While Rhonda rattled on, Helen whispered, "Here we go again," stating that toddler Ricky "ingested almost anything he could get his fat little fingers around." She'd earlier informed me that anyone within two blocks used Louise as the local healthcare helper. They regularly expected advice and emergency care, even more than they asked her husband for help with their cars.

Louise rapidly switched roles to reluctant rescuer. "Well, I guess I finally know what I'm doin' tonight!" she said with a shrug. Springing up, she trotted out stage right, grabbing a Syrup of Ipecac vial to induce vomiting. Rhonda followed.

Little Roy, silent again, headed back to his room.

Alone with her stunned guest, Helen turned off the television. "You enjoying the Campbell holiday shitshow?"

"Fascinating," I said, trying to assemble the circus into a meaningful whole. My weakness: the impossible conviction that one could make sense of any situation if one simply observed long enough. This turkey-story saga defied comprehension for me.

I leaned toward Helen, hoping for a kiss, interrupted by the return of the Neighborhood Nurse.

Louise tossed her puke-splattered smock into the laundry room and reclaimed her cigarettes — and spotlight. "These goddamn people around here don't have the sense God gave a goose! They let their stupid kids do stupid things and then 'spect me to fix it. They ain't good for doin' nothing but askin' me for another favor!"

"Mama, maybe you forgot your bookkeeper friend Rhonda does your taxes every spring — gratis," Helen smirked.

Act V featured weaponry. "Well, I'll tell y'all one thing. That sonofabitch I married better not show up tonight or he'll see what my little gun can do!" Louise said.

I gave Helen another worried glance.

"Oh, don't worry," she said. "Mama always talks that way when she's real pissed at him."

"He may find out different this time!" Louise retorted. Weeks earlier, she'd shown me the weapon, an aging .25 caliber pistol, but confessed she didn't know where to find the bullets.

"It don't matter," she continued, "I'm goin' to see Hap Lundgren on Monday!" Lundgren acted as the region's foremost divorce attorney.

"Yeah. Like you could afford him!" Helen laughed.

Booming knocks on the front door opened Act VI.

"Another neighbor with a sick kid?" I tried to joke.

"No. That's my asshole father!" Helen snapped.

"Don't let him in!" Louise yelled uselessly as we heard a struggling key turn the lock. Helen released my hand, curling up as would a child preparing for a beating, forearm protecting her left eye.

Louise's nostrils flared like a bull's. The volume from the bedroom, a Ginger Baker drum solo, rose. So did my adrenaline and fear. My left heel started involuntarily bouncing on the floor.

The door swung inward, pushed by a thrust of 40-degree air.

"Happy Thanksgiving, y'all!" Big Roy loudly beamed. He wore his dark blue work coveralls. I could faintly smell liquor, but he strode forward without staggering. He looked taller, maybe six-two, and stronger than I remembered — broad shoulders, long arms and large gnarled hands that showed the arthritic abuse of turning wrenches for decades. But an almost silly grin, combined with tousled red hair, made him less threatening than a moment before.

"Hi, Bill!" he said with a quick glance my way, then focused on Helen.

"How's my little darlin'?"

"Get away from me, you snake!" she shouted, eyes averted.

Ignoring Helen, Big Roy quickly turned toward his wife of 21 years, bowing his head. "I'm sorry I'm late for dinner, honey. I just got a little upset, ya know. So I went back to the shop. Finished up a Fairlane. I am really sorry this time. Y'all understan'?"

"Yeah, I 'understan' a shitload of lies when I hear them!" Louise fired back, clenching her fists.

Blessedly, I did not see her reach for a gun.

"Ah, come on. It's hardly seven o'clock an' it's time for dinner an' I'm as hungry as an alligator in a fish run. Sure smells like ya cooked up somethin' good, Sweet Pea!"

"Dinner's in the goddamn garbage. Serve yourself!"

"Hmm," he grinned again, as though he knew that answer in advance. "So, I reckon we'll have to jump di-rectly to dessert!" Big Roy returned to the front porch. His son stopped the music and returned to the party.

"Did I hear 'dessert'?" Little Roy chirped, his first full sentence of the night.

"Shut up!" his mother barked.

The man of the house reentered carrying a pricey Harris Teeter Grocery pecan pie.

He carried it like a restaurant waiter, a can of aerosol whip cream in the other hand. He then emptied the can on top of the treat. That monster in the aluminum pan weighed five pounds if it weighed an ounce. With a loud "Ta-da!" Big Roy ceremoniously, and gently, placed it on Louise's lap, proclaiming, "Now ain't you glad that beer bottle you threw didn't hit me?"

I couldn't tell if she would accept the offer or plant it on his face. Yet, there emerged a growing smile from what had been a hate-filled grimace. Her shoulders dropped as she leaned back in her chair.

"Well," Louise softened, "why don't you take us out first for a nice supper?"

"Anywhere, wife. Jus' tell me what ya'd like."

Louise's face glowed like she'd hit the jackpot on a dime slot.

"I want a steak an' baked potato!"

Mark Fryburg used to report broadcast news, practice public relations and teach people how to fly airplanes. A late bloomer (he's 74), Mark recently found new passion in writing and in performing live storytelling. Last year Mark took First Place in the Poetry Society of Virginia contest's "Sense of Place" category and Honorable Mention in the journal Passager's national poetry contest. This anthology presents Mark's debut short story. His love of story and journalism shows in his writing, which is likely concrete and concise (Mark aspires to be a favorite of readers with short attention spans). This Stanford grad lived five decades in his home state of Oregon. But the Blue Ridge always beckoned. In late 2022, Mark and his bride Laura retired to Virginia's Roanoke Valley, where they met more than 40 years ago. They reside, with two pups, in Daleville, Botetourt County.

CHRISTMAS EVE AT READ'S DRUG STORE

GARY SKAGGS

I fell in love with Traci McCullers in seventh grade. I fell out of love in eleventh grade — on Christmas Eve. Here's how it happened.

Read's Drug Store in Wise County, Virginia, is hectic when I arrive just before eleven. Last-minute shoppers angling for that one thing to complete the perfect Christmas morning eight hours later. At least the store is festive with strings of red and green lights hanging above the front door. Mrs. Warren, whom I'm about to relieve, has six customers in line. She's helping a gray-haired woman select a transistor radio. Four models lie side-by-side on the counter.

"My Roland can't read the numbers on this one," she says. "And this one's dial is too small. He's getting arthritis in his hands." The growing line of customers behind her looks skyward for deliverance. Mrs. Warren glances at the clock. She's anxious to make the midnight service.

The man next in line has only a bag of red and green M&Ms, so I ring him up. "Bless you," says the man. He races out the door. I take the next two in line when Mrs. Warren says, "Let me get the lady here." She's finally picked a radio. Mrs. Warren puts it in a paper bag and hands it over, just as the clock says eleven. She grabs her coat.

"Merry Christmas, Gerald."

"You, too," I reply.

Most of the remaining customers want cigarettes, magazines, or candy. I manage to shrink the line to two, but then an elderly man needs vacuum tubes for his TV. He hands me a brown paper bag of burned-out tubes of various sizes. The tubes are in a locked cabinet behind the candy display. I test each one by plugging it in its socket on top of the cabinet. Meanwhile, the line grows again like a weed.

"Anything else?" I ask the man.

"A carton of Pall Malls."

He pays me in quarters and dimes, counting them out one at a time. "Thank you, young man. You saved my Christmas." He looks at his watch. "Now I can watch White Christmas." I think about him spending Christmas alone with a movie and cigarettes and hope my life doesn't end up that way.

Traci McCullers is working the main register, just inside the front door. She examines her fingernails, checks her watch, yawns. All Traci has to do is ring up customers' purchases. People come to my counter for cigarettes, radios, watches, and other stuff that requires me to fetch and show and offer advice, in addition to taking money and counting change. But I'm not complaining. I've had a major league crush on Traci for four years. I enjoy watching her taking it easy. By midnight, I've worked my way through my line.

I can now give more attention to Traci. Dark hair, dark eyes, killer smile. That's what I noticed when she walked into our seventh-grade homeroom, her family having just moved from Indiana. She was super sweet to everyone. The combination of good looks and being nice was noticed by everyone in class, especially the boys. One day, she's gonna look like Elizabeth Taylor, they said. As for myself, I was too intimidated to ever speak to her. The following year, she was in a different homeroom and different classes. I lost track of her, except occasionally in the hallways, but I never lost the crush. Then, two weeks ago, Traci miraculously appeared as an employee at Read's Drug Store, where I'd been working after school. Dr. Read often hired high school students over the holidays. When I found out she'd be working the Christmas Eve night shift, I volunteered for the same. Dr. Read was thrilled. It's a hard shift to fill.

Traci is now wearing a lively sweater displaying Santa wearing a pair of strategically placed antlers. I can't tell if the sweater is meant to be provocative or just looks that way because of her body. I look up to find her looking at me. She waves me over. Here goes whatever.

"Sure was insane there for a while," she says.

"Sure was." A bead of sweat rolls down my back.

"Another hour, this place will be deserted. Then, we can have some fun." She laughs. "Dr. Drunk will be completely ripped by then. He won't care." Dr. Drake is the assistant pharmacist who works the night shift. We call him Dr. Drunk because a bottle of Old Grandad helps him get through the lonely dark hours. He's also Dr. Read's nephew. His job is secure. Read keeps him on night shift to minimize the damage.

Traci abruptly changes the subject. "You seeing anyone?"

The true answer is no. In fact, I've never even been on a date, but I can't admit this. She'd laugh at me. I say, "No one special. What about you?" She laughs, but it's a bitter laugh. "All boys just want one thing. Sometimes, I just want someone I can talk to."

My hopes rise when I hear this. Yes, I can be, I would like to be, a boyfriend who is also a best friend. I can do that better than any other guy. Why not ask her to go with me to the sock hop the school puts on every Friday night? I summon the courage. "Say, Traci — "

A man carrying aspirin and Rolaids comes to her register. I retreat to my counter, frustrated and relieved at the same time. Later, the store will be empty. I'll ask her then. After the man leaves, Traci pulls out a Look magazine and thumbs through the pages.

By two, the only ones in the store are Traci, me, Dr. Drunk, and two other students. Judy works the cosmetics counter, which has been crazy busy with men asking her what to give their wives. Tommy is a part-time custodian. He stocks the shelves, cleans the bathroom, sweeps the aisles, but spends most of his time in the basement, doing who knows what. The store right now looks like a war zone. More stuff on the floor than on the shelves. Tommy is working his way forward in the middle aisle, putting things back on shelves, not necessarily in the places where they belong. When he gets to the front of the store, he walks over to my counter. He pulls a pack of cigarettes from his shirt pocket and lights up. "It's gonna take all night to straighten out this crap." He takes a couple of restorative drags. "Hey, put something good on." He points to the eight-track player sitting on the shelf behind me.

I have no idea what Tommy might like. I insert Neil Diamond:

"Baby loves me, yes...

...girl's outta sight, yeah."

Tommy holds the cigarette in his mouth as he snaps his fingers to the catchy beat. He glances over at Traci, who's watching us. The song ends. While staring at Traci, Tommy says, "Play it again." I push the reset button. Tommy cups his hands over his chest and whispers, "Oh man, I want Traci so bad." As if she heard him, she smiles. Tommy checks his watch, looks around. "No one else here. Let's party! Go get Judy."

Judy is trying to read a paperback, but she looks nearly asleep. She sits up when I approach. "Hey, we're meeting at the fountain. Wanna come?"

"Okay."

Tommy and Traci are sitting side by side in a booth when we arrive. "Hey, Judy, can you make us cherry cokes?" asks Traci.

Judy subs at the soda fountain sometimes. She goes behind the counter. A minute later, she returns with four full glasses with straws.

"These are great," says Traci after a few sips. "Can we add something stronger?"

Tommy laughs. "Gerald, turn up the music." He stands. "And bring back cards and poker chips." Tommy heads toward the back of the store. Neil Diamond is still playing an endless loop. I turn up the volume and return to the booth. The cards and chips are both new. I'll need to pay for them but I open them anyway. Tommy returns with a plastic cup filled with Dr. Drunk's whiskey. He pours some into each glass, giving a bit more to Traci. We play poker until four. By that time, Judy is wiped out, me nearly so, Traci about the same as when we started, and Tommy has all the rest of the chips. Just then, a man in a dark suit enters the store and heads for cosmetics. Judy follows him.

Traci says, "Gerald, will you watch my register while I go to the potty?"

I stop by my counter. "Cherry, Cherry" is getting on my nerves. I replace it with Bing Crosby's Christmas tape. Back at Traci's register, I have a view straight out the glass front door into the parking lot. No white Christmas so far.

It's then I notice that Tommy is no longer sitting at the booth. A few seconds later, I think I know where he's gone. And twenty minutes after that, my suspicion is confirmed. Tommy and Traci walk toward me up the center aisle. They giggle and bump shoulders. She wasn't on any potty break. And just like that, the bubble bursts. I fall out of love.

"Did I miss anything?" asks Traci.

"Not a thing," I say. Tommy is grinning. We make eye contact. Tommy winks at me.

I return to my counter. I play solitaire with the deck I opened earlier. Around six, customers begin to enter the store. Traci rings up a steady stream of shoppers. I get a few. So does Judy. I get an occasional glimpse of Tommy keeping the aisles clear. At seven, Dr. Read relieves Dr. Drunk who staggers out the front door. The regular staff come in to relieve the students.

I put the cards and chips in my coat pocket, fish out two dollars from my wallet, and ring up my purchase. I'm ready to leave when I spot Judy coming toward me.

"Going home to open presents?" she asks me.

"Yeah." I'm not excited about this. "You?"

"It's just me and my mom. It's gonna be a pretty quiet morning before I take a long nap." I haven't thought much about Judy in the month she's worked at Read's. But now I notice that, behind the thick lenses of her glasses, her eyes are a pretty shade of blue. She says she has nothing planned for the rest of the school holiday.

I don't think, just blurt it out. "Would you like to go to the sock hop sometime?"

Judy answers, "Yes, I'd like that. When do you think?"

I'm an old man now. I've been married forty-five years and counting. No, I didn't marry Judy and live happily ever after. I did take her to a Friday dance. She was very nice, but the spark just wasn't there. It was another ten years before I met Lynn. Between Judy and Lynn were many starts and stops that didn't work out. And yet that Christmas Eve at Read's Drug Store in Wise County, Virginia, was a big moment in my life. I discovered how heartache can lead to something better. And so, by the time I met Lynn, I knew gold when I saw it.

Gary Skaggs is a professor emeritus at Virginia Tech, where he taught research methods in the School of Education for over twenty years. He authored many academic articles about standardized testing as well as the academic nonfiction book Test Development and Validation (Sage Publishing).
He is also a co-author of the children's picture book Bosco D. Beagle (KDP Amazon). When he is not writing

fiction, he enjoys tennis, hiking, and kayaking. He lives with his wife in Hardy.

How Leslie Saved Christmas

David N. Bethel

After dinner on Christmas Eve 2001, my family prepared to drive around Roanoke to look at yuletide light displays, a cherished holiday tradition in the Bolton household.

My wife, Melody, a kindergarten teacher for eighteen years at the turn of the millennium, had prepared the evening meal on December 24. Early in our marriage she and I established a rule: whoever cooks does not clean. Following our repast, I rinsed soiled dinnerware at the kitchen sink and loaded everything into the dishwasher.

Meanwhile, Melody heated hot chocolate in a pot on the stove. She had developed the delicious recipe herself. She planned to take the beverage with us, to help keep us warm on our drive.

Finished with the kitchen cleanup, I glanced at my watch. I noted the hour had not yet reached six o'clock. The sun had set around five p.m.

I stepped to an upstairs picture window. I peered out, checked a thermometer mounted on the rear wooden deck, visible in the glare of a porchlight. The temperature registered a chilly 35 degrees. By Christmas morning, the low would reach a frigid 23.

The hot chocolate heated, Melody poured the liquid treat into a tall Thermos.

At the coat closet by the front door, my family bundled into heavy outerwear to protect ourselves from the cold during our outing.

"Gilbert," said Melody, snug in a ski jacket, "I need to run down to the basement to get disposable plastic cups. While I'm gone, would you help the girls with gloves, scarves, and knit hats?"

"Sure," I said. I turned to my three daughters, bedecked in their coats. "Okay, ladies, step right up and select your preferred winter accessories."

A multi-pocket organizer hung from the rod in the closet. The pockets contained enough cold-weather accoutrements to outfit a horde of snow birds. Here in the mountains of Virginia, we kept plenty of such items on hand, because our beloved progeny had a propensity to lose them.

Middle daughter Lilli, eight years old, chose an attractive set of matching pink apparel. I helped her put on the gloves.

"Can I bring Cara?" she asked. Cara was Lilli's doll. Cara wore a beautiful ruffled gown. Lilli wore a duplicate larger dress. My youngster looked lovely, and particularly huggable, in her finery, though a parka now covered her clothing.

Lilli, the princess of our family, insisted on wearing a dress to school nearly every day of her childhood. When she entered junior high she joined the band, developed a preference for more practical attire, and the days of royal splendor came to an end. In later life she became, like her mother, both a teacher and a loving parent of her own trio of wonderful children; also a devoted wife to her Air Force pilot husband.

"Of course you can bring Cara, honey," I replied.

"Can I bring Rex?" requested six-year-old Lauren. The youngest girl had picked out gloves, hat, and scarf of clashing colors. I aided her while she donned her gay apparel, especially assisted with the troublesome gloves.

"Rex may come, too," I assented. "Does he like Christmas lights?"

"I don't know if he does or not, but I think they'll make him feel better."

Rex was Lauren's stuffed German shepherd. The poor little accident-prone pup wore a handmade bandage around an injured front leg. One always hoped the hapless canine would someday experience a protracted period of wellness but, sadly, when he wasn't suffering from a drastic disease, he tended to fracture an appendage. Attending to Rex's numerous health issues led Lauren into a future career in medicine — not as a veterinarian, as one might expect, but as a physician for human animals.

My eldest daughter, Leslie, a high school freshman, no longer required assistance with gloves and sundries. When fully accoutered, she extracted a cassette tape from a coat pocket, held it up in a gloved hand, and asked me, "While we're driving around town, can we listen to this tape I made? It's Christmas music."

Yes, friends and neighbors, this incident occurred so far back in history we still listened to cassette tapes. Five more years would pass before we owned a vehicle equipped with a CD player. Digital music? Hadn't even been dreamed of yet.

"Which Christmas music in particular?" I inquired.

"Songs we like to sing along with while we look at lights. You know, like 'White Christmas' by Bing Crosby; 'Blue Christmas' by Elvis; 'Jingle Bells' by Alvin and the Chipmunks. Stuff like that. Oh, and the 'Hallelujah Chorus'."

"You remember your mother and I love to sing the 'Hallelujah Chorus' while looking at Christmas lights?"

"Of course."

"Well then, we will certainly listen to, and sing to, your tape. Thanks for making it, sweetheart." I kissed my fourteen-year-old daughter on the forehead.

She grinned from ear to ear.

Melody joined us at the front door, Thermos and stack of cups in her hands.

"Okay," I said to my warmly dressed family, "y'all ready to hit the road?"

"Yeeeeees!" responded the youngest pair of children.

"Then let's go."

We headed out of the house.

The last to exit, I locked the front door by simply turning a button on the interior knob, and pulling the door closed behind me.

As we climbed into the Bolton minivan my eyes suddenly flew open wide. I realized I had made a serious mistake.

Oops! I thought.

I turned to my wife. "Darling, angel, love of my life," I said, "do you have your keys in your purse?"

"I didn't bring my purse," she replied.

Uh-oh.

"Why do you ask?" she continued.

"Because, sweet-ums, the apple of my eye, I forgot my keyring. I don't have keys to the car, or keys to the house. I don't have keys to anything."

"Oh no." My wife's happy expression collapsed. I saw it fall. The sight hurt my heart.

"We are locked out of the house with no way to get in, and we can't drive anywhere to seek assistance." I chuckled half-heartedly, said, "Merry Christmas."

"Maybe we didn't lock one of the back doors," Melody suggested, a desperate grasp at hope.

"Maybe," I said.

"Let's check."

Everyone exited the van.

The house is built into a hill. The top floor sits at ground level in the front, but it and the lower level are exposed in the back. We passed down the slope to the rear of the residence.

I climbed the concrete stairs leading up to the wooden deck off the kitchen, attempted to turn the doorknob on the kitchen door.

"Locked," I announced.

Melody checked the basement door at the bottom of the stairs. "Also locked," she said.

I rejoined her and the girls.

"What are we going to do?" Melody asked.

"Your aunt lives in town," I said. "We gave her a key to our house for use during an emergency. I'd say tonight qualifies as such a crisis."

"How are we going to contact her? My aunt doesn't live nearby. Her residence is several miles away, too far to walk."

"We could call her. I'd rather not interrupt a neighbor's Christmas celebration, but we could knock on one of their doors and ask them to let us use their phone." In the prehistoric era we wore bearskins, painted primitive pictures on the insides of our caves, and carried stone knives. We did not carry cell phones. Yet.

"We can't," said Melody with a sigh. "I just remembered. My aunt is out of town for the holidays."

Another idea came to my mind. "I could break the window on the basement door, reach inside, and unlock it."

"I'd rather not mess around with broken glass tonight. We will, though, if we can't think of something better."

"Okay. What then?" I asked myself. I glanced at the upstairs bathroom, directly above the basement door. "You know, the bathroom up there has never had a lock on its window. The lavatory is high off the ground and inaccessible. It doesn't need one."

"You're right. But we don't have a ladder. We'd have to borrow one from a neighbor."

"Yeah, and I prefer not to disturb anyone. Let me think a second."

I closed my eyes. I silently asked the Lord for His help.

When I opened my eyes, I saw the answer to my prayer right in front of me.

"The girls' swing set!" I proclaimed.

The swing set stood in the backyard, about thirty feet away.

"It's not anchored," I stated. In all the years my daughters played upon the apparatus — before and after 2001 — I never anchored it to the ground, our backyard far too rocky to do so. For the one and only time as a homeowner, I felt glad to reside upon rugged terrain.

"We can move it," I continued. "We can reposition the jungle gym here, directly beneath the upstairs bathroom. If we flip it upright on one end, I think the other end will reach the unlocked window. It's not strong enough to support me or you, Melody, but Leslie," I turned to my softball athlete oldest daughter, "I'm pretty sure it will hold you. If you are willing, you can climb up the center bar, push open the bathroom sash, and get inside the house."

Three metal A-frames supported the swing set, the legs connected to a long overhead bar.

We spread out around the structure, took ahold of it, and lifted. We immediately discovered the contraption to be surprisingly heavy, the five of us barely able to heft and carry it, yet we managed to place the apparatus where we desired. We even capsized it onto one end of A-frame legs, but — oh no! — the swing set wasn't long enough. It did not reach the bathroom window.

We stared at our failure, dejected, dispirited, defeated.

Leslie spoke up. "I can make it," she asserted. Her natural courage served her well in later life, in her profession as a police officer.

Melody, Lilli, Lauren, and I held the swing set as still as we could. Leslie ascended the upended playground equipment like Santa Claus climbing the inside of a chimney. Her agility, balance, and audacious confidence greatly impressed me.

When she reached the top, she stood unsteadily on a pair of A-frame legs. She could just reach the bathroom window with both hands raised above her head. No screen covered the glass. She pushed the sash open with ease but would have to jump to get herself through the casement. She paused, stabilized herself by gripping the sill, and evaluated how to go about the process.

"Be careful, honey," cautioned Melody. "Don't try it if you don't think you can make it."

"I got this," said Leslie.

"Watch out for the toilet," I warned. Inside the bathroom, the john sat directly beneath, and perpendicular to, the window.

"Here I go!" Leslie declared. She launched herself upward. Her head passed directly through the open window and she landed, with a grunt, on her belly on the sill. Stuck for a moment, she kicked her legs into the empty air behind her, which helped her wiggle through. She dropped into the bathroom and out of sight.

As the bottoms of her shoes disappeared we heard the toilet flush. We roared with laughter. Leslie poked her head out of the window and gave us a smile and a wave. We cheered.

We had a ball on our drive to admire Christmas lights. We sang along with Leslie's tape — particularly enjoyed adding our voices to the "Hallelujah Chorus" — drank every single drop of Melody's superb hot chocolate, and had a grand time. A few days later I installed a lock on the bathroom window.

Every year we tell the story of how Leslie saved Christmas by climbing a tipped-over swing set to gain entrance to the house through the unlocked upstairs bathroom window. And how she flushed the toilet on purpose as a joke.

David N. Bethel lives in Roanoke and has worked various jobs over the years from warehouse manager to processer of college student admission paperwork to Director of Operations for a local food bank. He is a member of Roanoke Valley Christian Writers and has written stories and articles for several Virginia publications.

CHRISTMAS WAS FOUR DAYS AGO!

HOLLY BRINJA

Chunks of sleet rapped against weathered window-panes and fell into a pile at the windowsill. By morning, they'd be frozen shut.

"Blow out those candles and get away from the windows," Ann directed her children. A gust sent vibrations through each plate of glass to emphasize her point.

"Where's Father?" Sarah screamed, jumping into her mother's arms.

Heavy boots crunched beneath the snow, muffled by the wind's sporadic cries.

"There he is!" Arthur yelled.

Sarah leaped from behind her mother and took off for the door. Her hurried feet tangled in her nightgown on the second step, and head over feet, she slammed against the door. Grasping at the doorknob, she rose to her feet. Less than an inch into the turn, a hard rap from the other side of the door sent her in the opposite direction.

"Let me in!" a deep voice said. "Please," he said more softly.

Both children looked at their mother. Forehead wrinkles wriggled across Ann's face, and she ushered them together. Arthur took the candle and his sister's hand to guide her up the stairs.

Halfway to the door, Ann looked back and found her children frozen behind the single flame. She rolled her shoulders, puffed out her chest, and closed the distance.

"Who is it?" she said.

"Please, ma'am, I got caught in this storm. My horse, I think, twisted his ankle. Please."

Ann's stance softened. She rested her head against the door for only a moment before she opened it and stepped back. Flakes rode in on the cold gust, littering her tight bun and stealing her breath with a sharp stab. In front of her was a man not much taller than herself, and behind him, his horse whined on the porch.

"Thank you," the man said. He didn't wait for a further invitation; he pushed past her and tipped his hat. "You're very kind," he said behind chattered teeth.

Ann closed the door but remained quiet as the stranger intruded. His eyes darted in each direction until his attention fell on the tall Prussian case clock. One finger drew a trail in the dust to an illegible brass plate. A smile spread across the man's face. When he removed his dirtied cuff, the word Spitler could be seen through coagulated dust. Without warning, he opened the face and tinkered for a quick moment. When he closed the door, the cogs ticked their first tock since Sarah was born. In awe, Ann stood between the man and her children. His eyes breezed over them; he bowed and retreated to the drawing room.

The three of them followed at a distance. The man picked up his pace and unwrapped his scarf, finding a place to hang it on the decorated hearth. Each layer he removed shrank his stature; by the time he warmed his hands in front of the wood stove, he'd lost fifty pounds.

"I can't tell you how much I appreciate this, Miss," the man said.

He shook out his shaggy hair. The ejected droplets of melted snow sizzled to vapor against the cast iron.

"I'm sorry to disturb the whole house," he said.

"It's fine," Ann said.

Sarah twirled one of her braids behind her mother and looked out the window. She whispered, "Mother, where's Father? He should have been back by now."

The man's eyes fixed on Ann.

"I'm sure he's alright. He's just somewhere waiting out this storm," she said. Loose strands of Sarah's hair slipped through Ann's fingers. "He went out earlier to bring home our Christmas tree," Ann continued. "We're a bit late this year with the sickness we've only recently overcome. He should have been back by now, but I'm sure he got caught in the storm like you."

The man looked delighted.

"Christmas?" He clapped. "What a treat! I haven't celebrated Old Christmas in years — since I was a child, come to think of it."

No one said anything, and the man placed his boots to dry near the fire. His toothy smile faded at their confusion.

"Christmas tree?" he repeated. "You are talking about getting ready for Old Christmas, aren't you?"

"Here, we just call it Christmas. Where did you say you were from?" Sarah said.

"Oh," he said. "Ohhhhh."

He sprang up, and his hands shot into his black trouser pockets. He paced and muttered and shuffled something around in the left pocket. Then he stopped and produced a marble, twirling it between his fingers. He mumbled a few more things, and his finger wrote them in the air.

"When was the last time you had a visitor?" he asked.

"This time of year? Never," Ann said.

"Huh," he acknowledged. "And no one has mentioned the calendar change during the warm seasons?"

"Calendar change? You can't just change a calendar," Sarah giggled. "Even I know that."

"Oh, but they did! Julian is out, and Gregorian is in. Christmas was four days ago!" He clapped again. "You folks are about to celebrate what has been dubbed Old Christmas. But it's been thought that the whole world knew about the calendar change by now. It's been over 200 years. How long have you lived here?"

"My whole life," Ann said. "My husband and I both grew up on the mountain. He comes from descendants of Phillips and I, Mabry."

"You don't say." He looked her over. He took a couple more paces, turned on his heel, and asked, "Does everyone up in Floyd still celebrate Old Christmas?"

"I'm not sure," Ann said. "I guess it's never been talked about."

Sarah piped, "Tell us more about where you're from?"

Ann scolded her daughter.

"The coast. Norfolk to be exact. A friend from my travels offered to let me assist around the farm in exchange for a room a while back. I find myself back in a bit of trouble, so I'm hoping to take him up on the offer."

"What kind of trouble?" Arthur said.

"Well, that is my own business." There was a long pause. "What would you folks be doing if I hadn't come knocking?"

"We were just retreating to bed," Sarah said.

"Well, please, don't let me keep you. I can tend the fire and keep an ear out for your husband. I'm sure I won't get much sleep myself; I want to keep a close watch on my mare."

Ann nodded and ushered her children up to their beds.

By morning, a thick blanket of snow hugged the house tight. Sarah sprang from her bed, wrapped her aged robe tight, and danced into her slippers. The warmth of the stoked wood stove met her at the cusp of the stairs, straightening her stance. Beneath her slender build, the steps creaked awake in protest.

"Stille nacht," she heard on the last step.

Sarah tiptoed across to the doorway. Her stomach lurched as she stepped through a curtain of apple and cinnamon. She peeked around the corner in time to see the man flip a fluffy apple stack out of the pan. It fell with a soft thud atop two others, and its steam joined their upward spiral.

"Holy night," he continued. "All has come." He faded off into a hum.

She watched in silence for a couple of moments.

"What's that song?" she said.

"Oh, hi there," he glanced over his shoulder. "Uh, it's a song I'm helping a friend translate."

Sarah climbed onto the couch and tucked her feet beneath her.

"How do you know German?" she asked.

He couldn't hide the surprise from his face.

She giggled. "Just because we're private doesn't mean we're uneducated. Mother and Father handle all our teachings," she said proudly, "and me and my brother are being given the same education." She sat up a little taller.

The stranger nodded, amused. "I learned it as a boy. From my father."

She smiled, accepting his word. Sarah leaned closer to the wood stove, inhaling as long as she could withstand, engulfed by the fragrances from the pan.

She rocked back and exhaled.

There was a crunch from outside. They looked at each other.

"I was just out for my horse and didn't see anything. She wouldn't be walking around, anyway."

The door flew open. A cluster of snow settled briefly and then melted on the foyer floor. Sarah squealed and ran to her father. Jumping, she threw her hands around his neck.

"Darling," he said.

"I'm so glad you're home," she said.

From above, fast footsteps paused at the landing before scurrying down the steps. Sarah was squished between her brother and mother within seconds. He had his big arms wrapped around all three of them. He gave an extra tight squeeze and they peeled off one after the other.

Sarah said, "Father, this is ..."

"Edgar," her father finished. "You didn't tell me you were coming!"

Holly Brinja, a writer originally from Pittsburgh, moved to Western Virginia in 2017 and has called Floyd home since 2021. She is the creator behind HB Creations, where she brings content and creative ideas to life. She most recently partnered with Andromeda Pictures, which adapted her story "(Un)Follow" for its 2025 short film competition submission. Her current work in progress, "Follow," is a preceding storyline based in the same world.

Opening Day

Todd R. Marcum

If you look at the calendar, there's no indication that the Monday before Thanksgiving is a red-letter day.

Yet the yellow buses slumber in their garage this Monday. Even if school were in session, the office would be flooded with tales of woe from drivers teetering at death's door. If the buses had drivers, there would be few students to ferry to school and hardly any teachers to instruct them when they arrived.

In Hamlin, West Virginia, Sunday night induces more insomnia than Christmas Eve, more prayers than a month of Sundays, and more reverence than Mother's Day. Buck season for firearms opens tomorrow at first light.

Twelve-year-old Chase slept fitfully in Pops and Mamaw's spare room. It was the same room his mother had grown up in. His dad was also an enthusiastic hunter, but Chase's family lived in an area lacking proper veneration for Opening Day. Since Dad had to work, he arranged for Chase to spend his first Opening Day with Pops.

Pops woke Chase up at 5:15. It was still a full two hours before the sun would break over the West Virginia mountains, but that was when Pops usually got up, so he saw no reason to deviate to accommodate his grandson.

Chase's grandfather was a retired Army captain. After a career in the military, he came home to Lincoln County with his wife and two girls, built a home on 30 acres of family land, and took a job at the high school, teaching math and coaching girls' basketball. With his military pension, he didn't need the money. He needed the purpose. He found it in teaching, in watching his girls grow to become women, get married, and have children. He found it in his farm, his church, and his family.

Lincoln County was a part of Pops, running through him much like the creeks that ran through the hollers. He was committed to sharing the land with his grandkids, of which Chase was the oldest. He had bought a Remington Compact for his grandson in preparation for deer season — the .22 Chase hunted squirrels with wouldn't bring down a buck — and the two had run the Remington through its paces as he taught the boy how to shoot it, to clean it, and handle it safely.

Chase was a good boy, a kind boy. Pops worried that he might freeze up when it came time to harvest a deer. The pair had been squirrel hunting, and Chase bagged a couple over the summer. He was a pretty decent little fisherman, too, but shooting a deer was different.

Pops cautioned Chase to stay quiet. How his mother had talked when she was Chase's age. When Chase's mom was a teenager, she had taken an interest in running with Pops, who kept up his PT for quite a while after his retirement. She would keep up a constant chatter regardless of the distance, speed, or terrain. Pops's ears got tired before his legs did. He missed those days.

"Pops, when you say I have to be quiet ... what if I have to go to the bathroom?" Chase inquired.

"Well, first, I do not have to be informed of your need to relieve yourself. As I recall, you've been handling that business on your own for quite some time now," said Pops. "But of course, we can talk if something needs to be said ... just keep your voice down. If you're talking, you can't be listening, and you're likely to hear a deer before you see one. I'm hoping we'll have some luck today, but how we behave can shift things in our favor."

There were plenty of deer around. Sometimes, you could count a dozen just by walking out onto the front porch, though Mamaw had a strict prohibition about shooting at a deer you could see from the house.

Still, there were no guarantees. The deer always seem to sense when hunting season comes around, and even a seasoned hunter could spend a day in the woods with nothing to show for it but an empty cooler.

At about a quarter after six, the pair loaded up the Gator with supplies and a cooler with a few cans of Diet Mountain Dew, Faygo Grape, sandwiches, and snacks and headed toward the deer stand. The stand was on Pops's property, and he liked it that way. It would allow him to peacefully enjoy Opening Day without worrying about other hunters.

Pops and Chase bounced along the gravel road about a half mile and parked the Gator beside a barn where the animals were sequestered. Chase tossed hay to the cows before the pair proceeded up the hill on foot.

Chase had to take two steps for each of Pops's strides, but he kept pace despite carrying the sandwiches and snacks. Pops had opted to pack guns, ammo, and drinks. Pops wasn't a young man, but you could hardly tell it the way he assailed the hill; buck season magic made his knees and shoulder hurt a little less.

It was still dark as the pair did their best to move stealthily up the hill, but their plan was thwarted by the abundance of leaves crunching under their footfalls. They reached the stand, climbed the ladder, and settled in for the wait.

It was a chilly morning, but the two settled comfortably. Pops had a sealed Tucker Tote with blankets. Between the blankets, jackets, and hand warmers, the pair were relatively toasty as they settled into their canvas camp chairs.

An amber glow crept over the mountains to the east, casting a glow over changing trees. When the sun broke over the horizon, buck season had officially arrived.

The two sat in comfortable silence, listening as the leaves that had managed to hang on rustled. Occasionally, they would hear a distant shot ring out. In his mind, Chase would speculate whether the hunter had felled a buck or missed. That wasn't fun for very long, though. Soon, he began imagining the hunter shooting at zombies, dinosaurs, and werewolves. His mind drifted to the things that occupy the thoughts of tween boys — video games, snakes, his beloved Cincinnati Bengals. At least half an hour ago, his grandfather started "resting his eyes" and was issuing a soft snore.

The boy was surprised at the ease with which morning flowed toward noon. From time to time, a shot sounded in the distance. Chase had moved on from imagining battles of mountain men versus Mothmen to listening to the leaves and the birds. The birds quieted down after a shot but must have short memories. They soon resumed their chirping.

A branch snapped somewhere down below, and Pops was scanning the forest in an instant. He crooked his finger to Chase. In the distance, Chase could see a doe with a fawn weaving through the hardwoods. The fawn was small, probably only a few months old — false alarm.

The pair broke out the sandwiches, with Pops enjoying egg salad while Chase had a PBJ, Faygo, and chips. They quietly spoke as Pops recalled their fishing adventures. Pops reminded Chase that patience was the key. With the sighting of the doe and her fawn, the morning hadn't been a complete bust.

The hunt resumed. After about an hour of thinking and waiting, Chase found himself staring at a log about 30 yards away, absent-mindedly daydreaming in a way that is rare for kids in today's era of cell phones and screens. The day was still chilly, though the sun had broken through the clouds and selectively punched rays through the canopy of maples and sycamores. The steady drone of nature, the weight of an early start, and the satisfaction of a full belly lulled Chase into a daze, the faint crack of distant gunfire barely registering in his mind.

Chase snapped awake as he heard the slow and steady crunch below the tree stand. Pops was already at the window, craning his neck awkwardly. Pops motioned to Chase, who slid over. Below, he glimpsed a buck, but it was still pretty far away, behind several trees and at an awkward angle.

Pops thought each sighting was like one of the giant Plinko boards he watched on "The Price is Right." The chip bounced this way and that, the contestant rooting for it to find its way to the big prize, but there was just as much of a chance it would go in another direction.

Similarly, there was a possibility the deer would pass into a line for a kill shot. There was a greater chance it would circle back, get spooked by a gunshot, or wander in the wrong direction. That said, deer hunting is about faith. So, they waited.

Pops motioned for Chase to get his gun ready but to keep it still. Anything from the platform's wood popping to the squeak of a camp chair could alert the buck to their presence and send it bolting into the woods.

The next 20 minutes were the longest of Chase's young life. Each second stretched as he watched the buck move with maddening slowness. His heart pounded, and he was acutely aware of every sound: the rustle of leaves, the faint whistle of the wind, even Pops's steady breathing beside him. It was like waiting for a math test to be passed out when you hadn't studied.

Slowly, ever so slowly, the deer crept closer. It turned to expose its flank. Pops helped Chase steady the barrel to be sure it didn't bump against the window and cause the buck to start. Chase lined up the shot. Pops held his breath as the shot rang out across the Lincoln County holler.

The deer collapsed in a heap. Chase let out a whoop. The two climbed down to be sure the shot had been true. It had. Pops hugged Chase tightly, the boy's radiant smile warming the crisp late-autumn day.

Todd R. Marcum is a Roanoke-based marketing consultant and creator who grew up in Wayne County, West Virginia. He is a recipient of the American Advertising Federation Silver Medal for lifetime contributions to the advertising industry and a member of the Marshall University School of Journalism and Mass Communications Hall of Fame.

His two books are Way Out Wayne and Baseball Cards at the Edge of War. He also wrote and co-produced "Shine: The Legacy of Roanoke's Advertising Men and Women," a full-length documentary capturing the advertising and public relations history of Southwest Virginia. He and his wife, Rhonda, have two grown children and are active community volunteers.

POETRY

GHOST   Tea Cart Art by Linda Thomas

Natale Villana

Annemarie Westphalen

1

Minor box turtle in mud I wallow
waiting for cold days to end.
Snow under the moon, what's left to know?
Christmas arrived both swift and slow;
no crystals in sky or ground to herald,
minor box turtle in mud I wallow
It rains for three days, four nights of woe.
On Christmas eve a full moon does ascend.
Snow under the moon, what's left to know?

The rain stops, clouds part in awe of her glow

as if God's light streams down without end —

minor box turtle in the mud I wallow.

When it rains through the sun we Anthropos

the devil's beating his wife again.

Snow under the moon, what's left to know?

Songs to make reptilians winter doze —

lullabies from mothers' mouths descend.

Minor box turtle in the mud I wallow.

Snow under the moon, what's left to know?

2

Little fox with black boots grinned

still behind the window, as the water under mists;

standing to scream, voice lifted on the wind.

Something beneath waited and watched —

Death is creeping up clips, chews, spits.

Little fox with black boots grinned.

Expanding to swallow my long lost friend,

between church bells and dinner bells Death shifts,

standing to scream, voice lifted on the wind.

Here you can observe the child dimmed.

Not me, never me. Pocketed hands, twists.

Little fox with black boots grinned.

Singing with rising tremored

voice and hands, in a Baptist wooden pew sweats,

standing to scream, voice lifted on the wind.

The candlelight service sees children gathered round

white beads of wax rolling through clenched fists.

Little fox with black boots grinned —

standing to scream, voice lifted on the wind.

3

Mama cat strutting through woods, fields, home —

when you couldn't see to drive through flakes —

only a memory, fading, fading, gone.

Napping like the ice-cream dome

atop peach cobbler at The Homeplace —

mama cat strutting through woods, fields, home

On those nights when boughs dome

and powerlines, from heavy crystals break;

only a memory, fading, fading, gone.

We gather round roaring fire, contained in stone.

Quilts stacked, legs akimbo, wide awake.

Mama cat strutting through woods, fields, home.

Too cold to play in the crick alone,

making snow angels beside the lake —

only a memory, fading, fading, gone.

Once I chased a kitten off the porch, overgrown.

Found her curled, cold, beneath fir tree ache.

Mama cat strutting through woods, fields, home.

Only a memory, fading, fading, gone.

4

Blacksnake winding through the mountains there,

snowdrifts up around either side of the track,

spy the Roanoke Star looming in the air.

Papa drives the interstate with care,

winter migration to Massapequa and back,

blacksnake winding through the mountains there.

From ya'll to youse like a prayer.

How will I know which is home I ask?

Spy the Roanoke Star looming in the air.

From youse to ya'll travel the contraire.

Reflectors his eyes — track our drive forth and back,

blacksnake winding through the mountains there.

Imagining you twinkle, twinkle my little star.

One if by land indeed cuts through the black —

spy the Roanoke Star looming in the air.

Rosy cheek pressed to cold tempered glass, peer

through to spy the moon smiling down on our act.

Blacksnake winding through the mountains there,

spy the Roanoke Star looming in the air.

Annemarie Westphalen grew up in Henry County. She was first published in A Celebration of Young Poets - Appalachia - 2003. Her work was also in Whatever, 2012, and The Album, 2012. She wrote a choral poem, "The Realism Behind Romanticism," for Best of No Shame Theatre, 2012. You can find her on Instagram @a.west phalen_poet.

Appalachian Christmas Carol

Kathleen P. Decker

from Merrie Olde England
comes the Cherry Tree Carol
Mary with child
Joseph with Mary
God with all
Says Mary the gentle.
"Joseph, please pick me
a sweet red cherry
from this great grove."

Growls Joseph the virgin husband.

"Have the father of your unborn child

pick you a sweet cherry,

I'm not in the mood."

Jesus works magic

from the womb,

bends the tallest, sweetest tree

to Mary's desire,

opens Joseph's stern heart

sways his earthly father

through his godly father

and the holy spirit

The blended tones

of Appalachian strings

proclaim the triumph of

this blended family

every Christmas

Dr. Kathleen P. Decker is an award-winning poet. She is a past president of the National League of American Pen Women, Seattle Branch, and serves as Vice President of the Poetry Society of Virginia, Eastern Region. She has authored several books of haiku, senryu, and tanka.

She has also authored western poetry books including Updraft and Fishmas: Twelve Days of Christmas by the Sea. She has edited four western poetry anthologies: Quilted Poems, Views of Virginia, Blended Voices, and Making the Unseen Seen.

MCAFEE KNOB AT NINE DEGREES

PIPER DURRELL

Pretty damn cold outside, we all agreed, with

smart wool socks pulled up, gators around our necks

three layers of inner outer wear, hats and hoods

sturdy boots tied tight, hiking poles held in hands buried in bulky gloves.

Cars and smart phones diverged as to the exact temperature —

perhaps nine degrees, give or take a few in either direction —

the forecast was: be forewarned as to a wind chill below zero a dire prophecy of frostbitten faces and limbs should we head up the path.

We debated and discussed but, after all, if decisions

are made by those who show up, then this was a group of stubborn women

whose votes had been cast when, at the winter sunrise,

their lunches were packed and loaded into backpacks

then, thrown into car trunks. Early.

The most determined of all had packed a thermos of wine and paper cups for the top.

Red. To be shared in a toast of conquest and friendship.

Attempts had been made in the past by the weather gods to ruin the plans

for an annual New Years hike to this mountain peak, and, truth be told,

the group had learned to be deterred by snow and rain and sleet.

But, mere cold was a force we could reckon with, helped by long johns and hand warmers.

The journey begins, hay foot, straw foot, trudging up the hill

on a rocky path with twists and turns, a tree to crawl over, roots to avoid.

Soon we meet a couple coming down, he informed us they'd been at the summit for sunrise.

How? We wondered. He said they had drunk champagne. No one asked, why?

Until they were out of earshot, when the questions were posed out loud.

Do you think he proposed? Did they take the fire road? Did they have headlamps?

For the next hour, or what the Fitbits claimed were the next two miles, no others passed us.

Conversations had then changed — our memories had promised this hike was flatter, shorter,

the camelback hoses were frozen, as were the chocolate bars, the Kleenex well-used,

layers had been taken on and off, now the clouds were coming in, the wind was blasting.

Coats were re-zipped, a lone hiker passed on his way down, "you're almost there,"

a slight exaggeration but an inspiring fib we chose to believe in, then

the trail marker right in front of our feet said otherwise but Jack the dog can't read

so he blazed his path up and over and through gargantuan boulders.

Eventually we all stood on the giant titled rock bump known as McAfee Knob, where

time may stand still but winds most certainly do not. Wine was drunk,

cameras were taken out, a stranger enticed by wine to take the group photo,

his frozen fingers steady on the camera, afterwards, one by one we tidied up from lunch, put the gloves back on, headed down.

Six miles, four hours of hiking, tired legs, backs, ankles, no frostbite.

Midafternoon the weary group emerged at the bottom with smiles,

a few minutes of hugs, then into cold vehicles where heaters were turned up high,

hats thrown into the back, each woman dreaming of warm showers and hot tubs.

New Years Day, 2018, an auspicious day on which to follow the advice of the wise John Muir —

"Of all the paths you take in life, make sure a few of them are dirt."

Piper Durrell moved to the mountains of Virginia in 1978 to work as an attorney at Legal Aid. She fell in love with the geography, the music, and the people. Most of her writing is based on observations of nature both here and across the amazing landscape of this country.

Epiphany & Advent Frissons

Molly O'Dell

EPIPHANY

It's a marrow cold morning, rime frost
spicules cling to most branches before
dawn. It's a day my skin demands no gaps
between shirt and britches, cuffs and gloves
or boots. The air is still but wet chill prevails
without luminosity. Every day I take
the same walk around town. Today's
upslope fog shrouds the northwest peak

called Purgatory. Along the way slush
starts to form where ice edged the road
when I set out. At the top of a long incline,
sun slips above the eastern ridge. Birdsong
swells and I glimpse white fluff from the tail
of a dear hopping deeper into the woods.
On my last stretch toward home, frost
melt forms expectant drops dangling
from thorns of a multi-flora rose bush,
now a chandelier. Each orb transfigures
light into splendor for any who choose to see.

Advent Frissons

Molly O'Dell

Not once does heron flinch
or preen or kick out her leg
tucked beneath blue-gray
feathers. We're routine guests
of this neighborhood run.
I walk all around
the elegantly perched bird
early after Germinids meteor
shower. My desire to be amazed
slaked by irregular darts, arcs & forked
streaks across the lonesome zenith
until they vaporize above kudzu
strangled trees out back.
Now blue heron preserves her posture
and watches decayed leaves float over
the creek where she fishes. She eyes
me then tilts her beak toward the water.
Not once does she wince
from fear or cold or dawn.

Molly O'Dell loves being outdoors. She received an MFA from University of Nebraska and has published a chapbook, Off the Chart; a multi-genre collection, Care is A Four Letter Verb; and Unsolicited: 96 Saws and Quips in the Wake of the Pandemic, written for her public health colleagues.

Clementine

Jessica Mardian

A peeled clementine,
half-eaten. Forgotten
as we hiked
the woods behind
your grandparents,
somewhere in the Blue Ridge.
Exactly where,
I don't know.
I get carsick and

have to focus

on the floor

as we fly

through backroads

that twist and turn

like baby ballerinas.

Jessica Mardian is a writer from Forest Virginia. Her work has been published in The Journal of the Virginia Writers Club, Red Cedar Review, Sunbow Zine, and Silhouette. Her poem "Tipping Point" won second place in the Virginia Writers Club 2023 Golden Nib Award. In 2018 she was a finalist for the Steger Poetry Prize. She studied Creative Writing and Multimedia Journalism at Virginia Tech.

ART

CHRISTMAS   by Linda Thomas

BRYAN SKINNELL

Appalachian Holidays

Bryan Skinnell has always had an artistic streak and enjoyed drawing as a kid but never harbored dreams, or desire, of becoming an artist. Being a pragmatic kind of guy, Bryan chose the traditional route of graduating from college (from the University of Kentucky). After graduation, he signed up for a tour of duty with the US Air Force. As a civilian again, Bryan worked in various jobs and vocations, and after years of drifting about, Bryan moved back to his hometown of Bedford, VA where he rediscovered his childhood love of drawing and making art. With that epiphany, life would never be the same. Bryan makes his living as an artist and illustrator in his hometown. He freely shares his life and adventures and, of course, his paintings and art on his website www.bryanskinnel.org.

CHRISTMAS CARTOON

PATRICK HARRINGTON

Patrick Harrington is a writer/cartoonist with a long career in advertising at agencies around the country.

For more info, Visit PatrickHarringtonCreative.com

An Offering of Gratitude

Kayleigh Scholes

Kayleigh Scholes is a Maryland-based writer, photographer, and podcaster. She often says that as a legally blind person, her art is how she chooses to see the world. Her work focuses on themes such as natural beauty, women, the human condition, mental health, and mythology.

By zooming in on these themes, she hopes to impart on her viewers a more nuanced perspective that gives them a clearer view of previously invisible beauty.

An Offering of Gratitude

STUFFED

MARJIE GOWDY

Marjorie Gowdy has pursued careers that fed her writing. Recent poems are included in Valley Voices, Indolent Books, Clinch Mountain Review, Artemis, the summer and fall/winter 2022 editions of Anthology of the Writers' Guild of Virginia, The Centennial Anthology of the Poetry Society of Virginia, the book Poetry Ink 2022 by Moonstone Press, and the 2022 book Quilted Poems. Her chapbook, Inflorescence, The Pasture at Rest, has been released by Finishing Line Press, March 2023 (Publisher Link). Also an illustrator, Gowdy lives, writes, and paints near Roanoke.

STUFFED

Tea Cart Art

Linda Thomas

Linda's interest in watercolor began in her 20s but was set aside as family and career took priority.

Many years later after family had grown and she retired from 30 years in banking, Linda rekindled her interest by taking classes from Harriet Anderson.

In 2016, after seeing Linda's miniatures displayed on a tea cart in her home, a local gift shop manager asked if she could display Linda's art for sale.

Since then, Linda has enjoyed creating her Tea Cart Art in galleries and shops from Southwest Virginia to Coastal North Carolina.

Linda resides in the beautiful Blue Ridge Mountains of Virginia with her husband, artist R.L. Thomas.

Appalachian Home

R.L. Thomas

Our Cover Photo

R.L.'s passion for art was evident early on with his report cards stating "his interest in art keeps him from his studies." He attended Richmond Professional Institute's School of Commercial Art and Design and has worked as an illustrator and designer in ad agencies and industry as well as founding his own ad agency in the 1980s.

After his retirement as a real estate broker for 20 years, R.L. began painting full time. His work is displayed in galleries in Virginia and North Carolina and his paintings are in private collections in the US and abroad.

R.L.'s work has been featured in "Best of Acrylic Painters and Southwest Art Magazine." He resides with his wife, also an artist, in the Blue Ridge Mountains of Virginia.

TRUE STORIES

Happy New Year   by Linda Thomas

Of Course We're Going to Grandma's for Christmas!

Audrey Garay

Our two tiny faces peeked around the mounds of colorful boxes piled around us. My sister and I were tucked onto a runner sled with blankets for warmth. My dad arranged his hat and tugged at his gloves. We were about to begin the mile-long sleigh ride to Grandma's house nestled in the rolling hills of Floyd County.

Snow wasn't, still isn't, scraped from the Blue Ridge Parkway, but my mother was determined that wasn't going to stop us from getting to Grandma's for the family Christmas celebration. Topping the hill, we could see the smoke, made by the three wood stoves, curling from the roof. Two potbelly stoves were used to heat the small shingle-sided house. The third one was a cook stove, used to prepare the scrumptious food we were expecting.

As we reached the bottom of the hill, the front door swung wide open. There was Grandma, dusting the flour from her hands on a cotton feed sack apron. After carefully navigating the two giant rocks that served as steps, we reached her outstretched arms.

In the kitchen, pintos were boiling. We could hear the rattling lid of a cast aluminum pot simmering a roast saved for the occasion. Freshly baked biscuits awaited the slathering of homemade butter that Grandma had carefully churned and pressed from fresh cow's milk.

Once inside, we removed our coats and helped carry all the Christmas gifts to the back room that was festively decorated with a limb. The limb, as my handicapped aunt called it, was their simple substitution for a Christmas tree. It was literally the bottom limb from a towering white pine tree, because there were no dainty, perfectly shaped trees on the land. The limb propped in the corner was decorated in fine array with a construction paper chain and a few plastic poinsettia heads. Grandma only had a small collection of plastic Christmas bulbs, probably not more than a dozen that were once purchased in a box.

When it came time to exchange gifts, Grandma's wish list was very simple. My mother prepared her a laundry basket of random gifts that would help her stretch the budget throughout the year. Things like lightbulbs, Scotch tape, ballpoint pens, freezer paper and masking tape were wrapped individually so that she would have a lot of presents to open. Sometimes Grandma didn't need a laundry basket. It was more important for her to have a new two-gallon galvanized bucket that could be used for milking or drawing water from the spring.

The grandkids always received a white envelope with two one-dollar bills carefully tucked inside. We understood the sacrifice even that was for my grandma. The adults only exchanged simple gifts, like cans of peanuts and boxes of candy.

When gift exchange was over, the adults moved into the "front" room and sat on the edges of two beds that flanked the walls to talk, while the kids stayed in the "big" room to goof around. The "big" room had one full-sized bed and a single couch, with a couple of cane bottom chairs scattered around.

Our ornery boy cousins threw oranges at us girls while we ate hard candy. There was the round, bumpy red candy that was filled with raspberry jelly and the little yellow and white rectangle candy that tasted like licorice. Yuck! There were the splendid colors of ribbon candy. My favorites were the green, yellow and orange ones that had citrus flavors. I didn't like the cherry red ones as much, even though they were pretty.

The cows didn't care if it was a holiday. Milking still had to be done twice a day, and there was a lot of wood to carry for heat and cooking. Grandma didn't get running water until I was almost a teenager. Even then, it was only cold. The water had to be carried from the spring under the hill, which was simply a bubbling creek with a board stretched over the creek where water pooled. The trick was dipping the bucket carefully for the water. Even though we wanted to rejoin the festivities, it was important not to dip too fast or deep because you would hit the dirt in the bottom and muddy the fresh water. A careless person could easily slip off the ice-covered board and end up a soaking wet mess having to trudge back up the hill with no water to show for our efforts.

Grandma lived off the land until finally reaching seven and a half decades. With gnarled fingers and a bowed back, strong-willed determination had carried her to the place that her heart had no more strength. At first the family felt the reason to go on was gone, but from Grandma's strength we were able to glean the fortitude to press onward. We learned to cherish the past and realize that Christmas didn't have to be about fancy bows and pricy gifts.

We had to take it upon ourselves to honor our Appalachian heritage and make each one of our homes the place where our families said, "Of Course We are Going to Grandma's for Christmas," because that is what love and families do. They gather, work hard, and treasure each other.

Audrey Garay lives in Bedford County, Virginia, with her husband, Steve. They have three grown children and nine grandchildren. They have been ministers for 25 years at Oakview Church of God in Roanoke. She works as an office manager at Mennel Milling. She is a codirector of Roanoke Valley Christian Writers and has just released her first novel, a cozy mystery, Secret of the Quilt.

A Tin of Christmas Magic

Arnette Crocker Tressel

While in high school I lived in the Presbyterian Home for Children known as Barium Springs. Each of us has our own perspective and memories of Christmas at Barium Springs, but for me one of my favorite memories is that of Ms. Taylor's homemade shortbread cookies. The first and only time that I tasted them I was marked for life, and my respect for the creator of those exquisite delights soared.

Ms. Taylor was the highest female authority figure on campus. To say that initially she seemed stern would be quite the understatement. Having arrived at Barium as a teen I had already developed a plethora of bad habits, and I had no respect for authority on any level.

I quickly learned that Ms. Taylor was my new guide to adjustment within the Barium structure. I learned that smoking in the underpass was not allowed. I learned that being late for anything was not allowed. I learned that everyone had chores and no one was more special than another. I learned my lessons the hard way and my heart filled with resentment for Ms. Taylor as a result.

But then one particular Christmas this trim, tidy lady with the heavy Scottish brogue stopped by Sanford Cottage and proudly presented a tin of magic: her homemade shortbread cookies.

Ms. Jackson, our housemother, knew the value of the visit, the tin, and the contents, and saw to it that each of us girls had a taste of the treasure. Each cookie was shaped like a little loaf of bread, thick with buttery sweetness.

As soon as my serving met my lips, I knew I had to make it last. I nibbled carefully, catching every crumb, savoring the texture, and studying the composition. As I ate, I swallowed my bitterness, and my heart filled with the sweetness of that moment.

Many years later, married with children of my own, I decided to try to replicate the recipe. I have found myself making them every Christmas now for 34 years. Though pretty close, my shortbread cookies are no match for Ms. Taylor's. But each year I still enjoy their preparation and sharing them with my family, and while I make them, I think about Ms. Taylor. I think about her devilish smile as she passed them around that first shortbread Christmas.

I think about the occasions later on while at Barium when I looked for and found her kindness; like the time when she requested our sizes for swimsuit shopping. I asked her if I could have one that covered more of my chest because I had a birthmark about which I was extremely self-conscious. She delivered the perfect resolution to my problem with the compassion of a concerned mother, and privately revealed that same warm shortbread cookie smile.

I guess I'll make shortbread cookies for as long as I am able; my children have grown to expect it. I hope they feel the magic, the peace, and the quiet contentment given to me by that first cookie. I hope they continue the tradition with their families.

It is a simple recipe and easy to follow:

- One-half pound of soft butter creamed with 1 and 1/4 cup of sugar.

- Add gradually 2 cups of plain flour.

- Stir with love and shape as you like.

- Bake for 15 minutes in 320-degree oven.

- Smile.

Merry Christmas and Happy New Year to all of you.

Rose Arnette Crocker Tressel is a retired media producer living near Smith Mountain Lake. She was born at the end of WWII of parents who worked for the Atomic Energy Commission in Oak Ridge, Tennessee. At age two, Arnette moved with her father to be near his family in Raleigh, North Carolina. Her Father's poor health led to her being placed in a home for children near Statesville, NC. She attended Peace College in Raleigh and later Roanoke College. Her avocations have included vocalist/musician, photographer, graphic artist, and voiceover talent for radio and television.

Halloween in the Mountains

Jen Heartway

My grandmother, Ida Mae, was a creature of habit. Born in the coalfields of West Virginia near the Tug Fork River, her life had not been easy. Her father was killed in a coal mine before she turned five, and her mother moved the family to Sparta, North Carolina, shortly after his death. The routine she cultivated after retiring from the pipe factory brought comfort and familiarity.

To the grandchildren who would spend the summer with her, she provided a predictable routine: same meals, same schedule, same activities. Every afternoon was spent on the front porch with a snack of Coke and peanuts, and that's when she shared stories. My sister and I would sit and listen as she talked about growing up in the mountains.

We tried to imagine a younger version of the woman who sat before us with snuff in her cheek. What was she like before she met my Grandpa (a Primitive Baptist preacher) and before she birthed five children at home? We couldn't imagine her as a mischievous teenager.

One day, Grandma looked around to see if anyone was listening before her voice dropped, and she began to tell us the story of the tricks she played on Halloween.

"Halloween wasn't like it is now," she said. "We didn't dress up and go trick or treating, but boy did we play tricks and try to keep away from the boogeyman and haints around the graveyards."

And her low chuckle carried across the yard.

"One Halloween when we was teenagers, me and Millie and Georgie went down to the cow pasture. We couldn't drive and if we could, we didn't have enough money to buy a car, so we walked there when the sun went down."

My sister and I looked down the road and imagined the pasture where the Williams family kept their cattle. It wasn't that far, but too far to imagine going there at night on Halloween.

"Back then, we would play all kinds of tricks on Halloween. Some were funny, but some downright dangerous."

We giggled then, because the thought of Grandma doing anything dangerous was outlandish.

"That Halloween we unhooked the barbed wire fence and stretched the wire all the way across the road."

"Did the cows get out?" I asked, knowing how hard it could be to get them back in if they started to wander.

"No. They were in another part of the field. That ain't the only thing we did. We got big ol' rocks and carried them out to the road for people to run over."

At this we gasped and looked quickly around for my grandfather. He loved his vehicles more than anything else, carefully cleaning and polishing them each week. Did he know she did this? How did he feel about her intentionally trying to damage cars?

"And after we finished with the rocks," she continued in a whisper as we leaned in closer, "we ran back home laughing the whole way!"

"Grandma! What happened? Did it break someone's car?"

"Oh no, it was much worse than that. It was worse than we could imagine. A little while later our neighbor, Earl, showed up at the house. His face was white as a ghost and he said there had been a bad accident. Earl said that someone driving down the road had hit the rocks and then drove into barbed wire. The wire had sliced his head right off and the head had rolled off in the field."

Mouths hanging open, like fish trying to gulp air, we stared at her.

"We was so scared we wanted to run and hide, and then Earl laughed so loud the whole house shook. He was just cuttin' up. He knew we'd been messin' with the rocks and the fence. He'd put the fence back together and thought it would be a good time to teach us a lesson. We never played a trick like that again. We never had anybody play a trick on us like that either ... except maybe your Daddy, but that's a story for another time."

Jen Heartway is a teacher, naturalist and author born and raised in the Appalachian Mountains. She lives on a small farm in Southwest Virginia with her husband, four children and unruly animals.

SEA OF SNOW

ANNE MARIE HAWKE

The beauty of the snow eclipsed the ugliness of our dysfunctional family, and for those few hours my sensitive heart was at peace. For the past two days the snow had fallen without ceasing in the Catskill Mountains surrounding my small hometown in upstate New York and turned the landscape into a winter wonderland. The snow clung to the trees like frosting on an electric beater blade, and the ground was a sea of pristine white crested waves. The roads remained untouched and the quiet of the beauty all around us could be felt.

I don't know who suggested we all go out into the snow, or perhaps it was merely the pull of the sublime. Either way we all put on our snow gear and began one of the most perfect memories I have as a child. We walked through the snow like we were walking on another planet where everything was new, and light, and fun. It was somewhere near Christmas, because we were all there: all six kids and my mom and dad. My oldest sister was home from college, and my oldest brother was back from military school for the holidays.

We walked and laughed, pulling down low-hanging tree branches as we went, dumping snow on each other's heads. We stopped and made snow angels. We had a huge snowball fight. We didn't see anyone else the whole time we were outside. It was like we were the only family in the whole town. It was a very special time, made extra special at the joy of having my mom there with us. She wasn't one to 'play' much, and I have very few memories of her coming outside to join in with whatever fun we were having beyond the four walls of our house. But that day she was bright-eyed and completely immersed in the beauty and wonder of the sea of snow.

To me it seemed like hours as we journeyed down the road on our side of the river. I was probably nine or ten years old that winter and I just loved every second of our magical walk through the snow. There was no one picking on me or finding some new way to torment me. There was no anger or indifference. It was just all good, good in the way a child should feel all of the time: safe, protected, loved, and cared for.

I think for most of my adult life I have been searching for that same serene place and never finding it. I have caught glimpses here and there in my children's smiles and laughter, in games played and stories made up, in times of seeing or experiencing beauty, in a gentle touch, in a warm embrace. But mostly this life has been one of pain and sorrow, hardship and yearning.

When I experience a serene "sea of snow" moment here I am thrilled, and I delight in it as long as I possibly can. But I yearn for a time when it will no longer be a fleeting feeling but rather a permanent reality. My heart aches for a heavenly shore on a sea of glass, where the streets are paved with gold, and everything is more than that wonderful winter walk could ever be. A place where I will be safe, protected, and cared for forevermore. Until then I have my memories and my hope to lead me home, to a place of no more sorrow, no more pain, no more death, and no more sin ... where at last I will see Christ Jesus in all His glory and be embraced by a love that knows no end.

Anne Marie Hawke has self-published a book of her poetry, as well as her first children's book, The Wee-Dunkers, and has several other writing projects underway. She has written a non-fiction work, Rescued, Redeemed, Remade: Rising Out of an Abusive Past. She owns her own business in Roanoke and loves reading and writing.

ALL I WANT FOR CHRISTMAS ...

JUDY JENKS

Every year I asked for a horse for Christmas. I was horse crazy from my earliest memory. I talked incessantly about horses to anyone who would listen, as if declaring my adoration would manifest a horse in my yard. A child's magical thinking is not to be reckoned with.

Living on 75 acres, one would think we would have horses. But our land was a mountain in central Appalachia. The woods, where I caught crawdads in the creek and picked wild berries, started mere yards from our front door. We had a large garden and cleared land for a yard, but horses need pasture and fence, and we had neither. Those details were hard for a five-year-old to understand; I simply wanted a horse.

My first day of first grade, I met a girl who had horses and offered to let me ride. In that moment, surrounded by new faces and the overwhelming smell of chalk in a one-story elementary school surrounded by farmland, I was starstruck. This girl had a horse. Pleading relentlessly spurred my parents to let me visit my new friend, and my eyes grew big as horse hooves when she led two ponies straight to me. Suddenly, I was face to face with a live horse, while visions of Bonanza and Gunsmoke danced in my head. She introduced me to a palomino Shetland named Trigger, and to Blaze, a dappled pony sporting a blonde mane and tail.

My friend's father handed Trigger's reins to me and gave basic instructions on how to ask her to turn, make her go forward, and how to stop. It seemed simple enough, but I abruptly realized this animal did not operate like a car when they cautioned that Trigger likes to rear up and slide the rider off her back. The pony, used to the clumsy coordination of children who can't ride, was much smarter than the little people who rode her. Suddenly, unexpectedly, I was intimidated. Befuddled, I decided that petting the pony was enough. But that was not to be; the grown-ups were putting me on a horse.

On my first attempt to mount the pony, the saddle slid under Trigger's belly and I fell to the ground. Trigger, cleverly, had learned to take a deep breath when the saddle was cinched so that the girth would be loose. The saddle was tightened and I tried again, but I accidentally kicked Trigger while slinging my leg over her back and she took off at a fast trot, with every stride propelling me out of the saddle like a jack-in-the-box and back into the saddle with a teeth-jarring bounce, until she veered sharply off to the side slinging me out of the saddle with the centrifugal force of a county fair carnival ride. I caught a glimpse of my friend catching Trigger by the reins as I lay on the ground catching my breath. At this point, I was done with this pony. But the prevailing echo from the grown-ups was that when you fall off a horse, you've got to get right back on.

I clutched the saddle horn again and pulled myself over her back, avoiding touching her body at all costs. I tentatively kicked her sides and she stepped out calmly, but I didn't trust her. I walked her around the back yard with an understanding beyond my six years of life that I had to keep this pony away from the clothesline or end up looking like the Tasmanian Devil in a tornado. She seemed content to follow Blaze until my friend dismounted; then Trigger had enough and promptly pulled her signature move of rearing up and dumping me on the ground. This time as I lay on my back trying to catch my breath, I stared at a cloud slowly morphing into Snoopy and thought that maybe getting a dog was a better idea.

As we drove home, my parents chattered cheerfully as if the pony escapades would break my horse fever. But I soon forgot the messy mishaps and my intensity escalated — I had ridden a horse! I had been thrown off and got back on! If it was true that you have to fall off a horse seven times to call yourself a rider, I only had four more fall-offs to go!

And so, when Christmas rolled around, I asked for a horse. And the next Christmas, I asked for a horse. My dad, in an attempt to maintain the sanity of the household, built me a wooden horse out of 2x4s and plywood. I rode Woody until one stormy night I heard a clatter and the next morning saw the wooden horse battered as if by Wile E. Coyote himself.

Again, I asked for a horse for Christmas. But the lack of pasture and fence did not fix itself, so my parents signed me up for riding lessons. Excited but tentative, I realized the horse waiting for me was taller and the ground a lot farther away than on Trigger. The saddle was smaller, didn't have a horn, and I was handed a helmet. I wasn't sure how I was going to mount this horse and I surely hoped he didn't know the trick of holding his breath when the cinch was tightened. I noticed the instructor carried a long whip and I wasn't sure if it was meant for the horse, or for me. They taught me proper seat, steady hands, and how to post a trot to eliminate the bounce, which my dentist greatly appreciated. I was tasked with grooming the large beast and saddling him myself by standing on a block. This horse was sophisticated, but I learned that the evasive veer to the side was a school horse standard, only now, I wasn't thrown off as often. To my nine-year-old self, this was marvelous.

By the time I was ten years old, my family frequently camped at a park that offered horse rides and my parents knew they could find me hanging around the hitching post. I was drawn to one horse in particular, a scruffy bay with a star, named Commander. I rode him every time I could talk my dad into paying for a trail ride. Before long, the park put me to work. I helped catch the horses, groom and saddle them, and lead the herd to the hitching post. Soon, I was helping with the trail rides, and I always rode Commander.

That Christmas, I again asked for a horse, but was old enough to understand why I couldn't have one. There was no place on our mountain land, nor the money, for a barn and fencing. Our little cinderblock house at the base of the mountain had four rooms on the main floor. The bathroom that Dad built after burning down the outhouse was so small that you sat on the edge of the clawfoot bathtub to wash your hands in the cast iron sink. The hallway was a square around the furnace grate. My bedroom was the ante at the base of the stairs that my three brothers had to pass through to get to their two attic rooms.

Every Christmas Eve, to keep us from spying on the presents, Momma hung a quilt in the doorway of the hall. But every Christmas morning, I woke early, peeked around the quilt and promptly ran up the stairs to jump in bed with my brothers and tell them what Santa had left around the tree. We lay in anticipation until we heard our parents stirring and we would bound down the steps. The Christmas tree, lit up bright against the darkness of the windows, held Santa's unwrapped presents scattered around the base.

Dad recorded silent home movies with an 8mm movie camera, the light so intensely bright it blinded anyone he aimed it at. We have years of Christmas morning films, us kids shielding our eyes every time we were instructed to show our presents to the camera. Afterwards, my brothers and I would sit around the tree comparing gifts, while Mom prepared Christmas breakfast. The weak winter sun would warm the pine wooden floors as it streamed through the windows, and later we would go sledding under the moon while Dad tended a bonfire at the top of the ridge.

The year I was ten, Christmas morning was the same, until Momma called us to breakfast. Dad followed behind with the movie camera, and like a moment out of the movie A Christmas Story, lying on the kitchen floor was a brand new western saddle! My eyes twinkled like St. Nick himself! My very own saddle! Under the laser-beam of the camera light, the saddle almost glowed. I ran my hand over the smooth leather and imagined how grand it would look on a horse.

By now the camera light was radiating heat like a stove eye but the warmth I felt inside made my Christmas complete. Or so I thought. Like a Hollywood director, Dad instructed me to look outside, and I flew with a flash to the back door. In the predawn dark, to my wondering eyes appeared something with long ears tied to the Shasta camper by the porch. I laughed when I saw it, in spite of myself, and with great delight, spun around and yelled, "You got me a donkey!"

I ran outside barefoot to see this remarkable donkey. But it wasn't a donkey, it was a horse. And not just any horse, it was Commander. As the day dawned I looked around our snow-dusted mountain and wondered where I was going to keep my horse. Dad explained that he had made a deal with our neighbor to let us pasture Commander on their property. In that moment, standing by Dad and looking at our small home tucked in an Appalachian holler, I decided that Santa brought me Christmas presents, but the love of my Momma and Daddy were what made dreams come true. I knew they would be there when life threw me off, no matter how far it was to the ground.

Judy Jenks is a native of Appalachia from Southwest Virginia. She is a Nurse Practitioner specializing in rural health and is an Associate Professor of Nursing at Radford University. She holds a post-graduate certificate in Appalachian Studies. She enjoys kayaking and hiking. She is a published photographer and author of creative nonfiction, humor, poetry, journalism, and academic writings.

Thanksgiving Snark

Georgianne Vecellio

It was a Thanksgiving long ago, and I had just clawed my way out of a crippling depression following the death of my dad, plus the deaths of several other family members and family friends. Frankly, I wasn't feeling thankful for much. While my mom was thankful for her family, I was coming to terms with the fact that most of the ones who were left were those I didn't like very much.

We were at our routine Thanksgiving meal at my aunt Carrie's. The one cousin I am fond of was spending the holiday elsewhere, but at least my cousin the criminal was absent from this gathering. I could at least be thankful for that.

I was lost in my own world, mindlessly munching on the holiday meal, when the other guests launched into the required compliments to our hostess.

"Oh, Carrie! You've outdone yourself!"

Hold on. I scanned the table and recognized the standard fare: corn, straight from the freezer to the microwave to the table; stuffing straight from the box; lumpy mashed potatoes; thick, jarred gravy—all the foods required for the holiday. Then there was the turkey.

"This is the best turkey ever!"

"It's so juicy and delicious!"

Wait, what? I took a bite of turkey and chewed it thoughtfully. Huh. I looked to see if other people had a special seasoning, but no, everyone was eating their turkey as served, with gusto.

I had always thought that you "had" to eat turkey on Thanksgiving, in commemoration of the first Thanksgiving (which might not even be historically accurate). I didn't realize that some people actually like turkey. I took another bite, enjoying neither the taste nor texture that filled my mouth.

At that moment, I had an epiphany, and I admitted to myself: "I don't like turkey. I don't like meat at all. I'm a vegetarian!"

Unfortunately, I uttered that last sentence out loud. My family was not amused, especially Carrie.

For a split second, I worried that Carrie might think it was her cooking that prompted my revelation. I quickly got over it—she might not appreciate my honesty, but she could handle it, especially since everyone else was heaping on the praise like they had heaped food onto their plates.

Then I had another realization: Carrie didn't actually like most of the people she invited to share her holiday meals, doing so primarily to be praised for her generosity, cooking and hostess skills. After a year of losses, that insight didn't faze me. I decided that I didn't have to spend my holidays at a performative feast filled with foods I didn't enjoy.

That was the last holiday I spent at Carrie's. I don't miss the turkey.

Georgianne Vecellio has written several Roanoker Magazine articles. A transplant to the Roanoke area, she now celebrates Thanksgiving with her in-laws and doesn't complain about the food. Mostly vegetarian, she has been turkey-free for over 20 years.

I Just Want to Dance

Bob Schmucker

"It was an absolutely amazing event and so many people in the community came together, and there was so much happiness and so many tears and so much surprise, strangers dancing without a care in front of each other."

Text message from Heather Rousseau

"I just want to dance" was Jenya's texted response when asked for ideas for the Christmas party that 3rd Street Coffee House was planning, to welcome her and her son Egor to Roanoke. Earlier, we'd asked if they "could use any Christmas love and support to replace whatever they had left behind in Ukraine." She suggested a couple of inexpensive toys for Egor and added that she didn't need any presents for herself, but just wanted to meet some new friends.

They had come a few months earlier as refugees from the war in Ukraine. A new country. A new language. A new culture. And, if that wasn't enough, her homeland and all that she loved had been invaded and occupied by the brutal Russian army. It had to have been overwhelming.

In December of 2022, the Roanoke music, business and Ukrainian communities came together to hold a Christmas party at 3rd Street Coffeehouse. The vision was clear: throw a party, invite a bunch of young thirty-somethings with young kids and Jenya could meet people. Add in kids and some games, and maybe Egor makes new friends too.

Jenya and Egor represented all the Ukrainian people who had been brutally attacked by Putin's Russia. The Christmas party was one way we could personally show support for the Ukrainian people. We all felt like this was way more than just a Christmas party. It was a multicultural, multi-ethnic, mixed bag of pizza, games, dancing (with a DJ), Santa and Mrs. Claus and lots of presents.

It was perhaps the best Christmas party I've ever been to. Strangers came together to welcome Jenya and Egor to Roanoke. Businesses donated food and all sorts of gifts. Volunteers jumped in at every step. It came together as though a higher power was guiding all of us — kind of a Christmas miracle.

In true miracle fashion, life-long friends and relationships were formed that day. Egor and I connected with high fives and winks, which led to hockey games, baseball games, ice cream trips and fishing. He's the bonus grandson I never knew that I had. Jenya became the bonus daughter I didn't know I had, and I became a bonus dad for her. They've both been a real blessing to my life even after they returned to Ukraine.

That day, I also made a lot of new Ukrainian friends, whom I have since become close to. Each of them has an amazing story and a deep love for their homeland. They've enriched my life in countless ways. Many of them were just learning English that day, but it didn't matter. Love is a language that everyone knows, as is the spirit of Christmas. Jenya said it best in a Facebook post:

"A miracle happened to us yesterday. We plunged into the atmosphere of love and kindness, which was presented to us by the inhabitants of Roanoke. People we did not know and never saw surrounded us with care and support. They showed how they support our country and our people. There were treats, gifts, surprises, games for children, children's laughter. There were tears and a moment of silence for Ukraine. There were new acquaintances and feelings of care and support. Thanks to all the people who passed and gave us gifts for postcards and kind words. Thanks to our new friends. This day will remain in my memory forever. Happy Merry Christmas and New Year for everyone. With love, our family."

Bob Schmucker is a writer, blogger, and community advocate. As manager of 3rd Street Coffeehouse, a traditional music venue, he has spearheaded numerous successful fundraising campaigns. He is an active member of several local writer's groups as well as The Southwest Virginia Songwriters Association. Recently, the city of Roanoke honored him for his significant impact on the local arts scene.

Christmas at Grandma's

Steve L. Garay

It seems like anywhere I go I end up in trouble. Hence the moonshine still across the creek. Christmas at grandma's should be fun, not hazardous.

My wife's grandmother lived on forty-ish acres land-locked by the Blue Ridge Parkway in Floyd County. Every Christmas we'd gather in her tiny five-room house. Three rooms downstairs and two small bedrooms up-stairs. She had raised nine kids as a young widow of 38 in this small house. Everyone was expected to show up for Christmas. Each brother, sister, aunt, uncle, cousin, nephew, niece, friend, and anyone else that showed up, crowded into that little house with shingle siding. Two pot belly stoves and a wood-burning stove in the kitchen kept the house more than cozy.

Walking in the door, you'd see grandma at the wood stove preparing dinner. Pots and pans covered the top, and a ham was in the oven. Green beans, corn, pinto beans, and potatoes. Biscuits sat on the counter and there were leather britches hanging on a string behind the stove, drying. Grandma's cheeks were red from the heat, and a bandana held her hair back. With a smile for everyone, she always wore an apron that fell to her knees. Even though grandma had little in material things, she always prepared plenty of food and had a little gift for everyone.

All of us grabbed a mismatched plate and dived into Christmas dinner. It didn't take long for some cousins to make a mess. But that's part of Christmas. Gifts came next, bringing joy to grandma's face, which was contagious. For me, the house was too full and too hot. I decided I needed to go for a walk. Pulling my wife aside, I explained what I was doing, gave her a kiss, and took off.

I enjoyed going to grandma's house. But escaping the crowd was a relief. Junked vehicles sat in the field with cows grazing around them. I took off down the hill, past the garden toward the creek. It was cold out but I enjoyed the peace. When I got to the creek at the bottom of the hill, I turned left and followed a faint path. I'd been walking for thirty minutes when I glimpsed the moonshine still.

I went down on one knee behind a tree to look for the owners. Moon-shining was a serious business and I was aware they would not be happy with me being here. I wondered if this was where my wife's uncle got his moonshine. Everyone in the family went to him to get a quart of shine.

A light haze hung over the moonshine still. I didn't know if it was from someone using the still or the creek. If there was someone there, I couldn't go back the way I came. I couldn't lead them to grandma's house.

As a hunter, I knew how to move through the woods. I circled around where the still sat. The leaves were damp, which made it easier to move quietly. A noise caused me to freeze behind the trunk of an oak tree. Movement attracts the eye, so I stood and listened. I couldn't tell if it was a person or a squirrel. I was not going to take a chance. After standing for a long time, I moved again, finding a trail; I started jogging. Between jogging and walking, I covered some distance. Losing track of time, I kept moving. I saw no one. Finally, I came out onto a road. I called my wife and asked if she could have one of her uncles pick me up. The family picked on me for "getting lost." I didn't tell them about the moonshine still. Some of the cousins would have tried to find it. When we got home, I told my wife what happened.

That little house burned down many years ago. Grandma's gone; Christmas memories remain. My wife and I visited the old home place in the fall. We picked some Ben Davis apples from a tree just below the old homestead.

Does the old moonshine still remain? I wonder?

Steve Garay has been married to Audrey for almost 43 years. They have three children and nine grandchildren. They have pastored Oakview Church of God in Roanoke for 25 years and are Co-directors of Roanoke Valley Christian Writers. He wrote travel articles for The Senior News for several years and has written two books and many short stories.

THUMBING HOME

DAN SMITH

I didn't have to go looking for Carl. Just listen for a minute and he'd show up, jabbering in a language he and about two others understood. And there he was, in the middle of five Cranberry High School students emptying out from the ancient stairwell that led to the top floor.

"Hey, Carl," I said too loudly, trying to get his attention. "Wanna go home with me for Thanksgiving?"

He didn't even think about his answer. "Yeh, man, we go Ah-ville? When we go? I need get un-wear and toot-brush. I be back in hour."

"Hang on a minute. We don't need to go until Wednesday, so you got two days to pack your underwear and toothbrush."

"I need fi minute," he laughed. "We see you mama? I like you mama. She like me."

That was the unvarnished truth. My mother adored this unbearably handsome Cherokee with a black mop of hair, bulky muscles and a smile like an airplane landing light. I probably should have been jealous, but that never popped up. Carl was simply too … well … Carl.

Carl Waycaster was an 18-year-old junior, a couple of classes behind where he should have been at his age, but he was not like the rest of us at school, in any respect. He didn't have a permanent home. He worked picking beans when it was warm outside and did odd jobs otherwise. He stayed where he could find a pillow, or in a car's back seat, on somebody's carpeted floor, or a soft natural bed in the woods. He showered at school and ate when he could. I never saw him unpresentable or down. He was always freshly scrubbed, always cheerful, always anticipating Another Great Day. No wonder Mom loved him. She understood him because she grew up poor and lived her life in that dark room.

Carl and I met on the football field in the fall of 1963. I was new to the school and he'd grown up with it. Our introduction was brief and violent when he tackled me as hard as anybody ever had, and the ones whose tackles I remembered were 50 pounds heavier and six inches taller than he.

I was a tailback in a single wing offense — a quarterback, in effect — and Carl played wherever he wanted to play on defense, mostly in the middle because he could see all of the field from there. I don't remember anybody ever giving Carl instructions about how to play or where to be at any given time. One doesn't correct success.

Ask Carl his position and you'd get a quick indecipherable "de-fent!" That was "defense" in Carl-speak. And it was as precise as Carl needed to be because that's what he played, all of it. He might sack a quarterback on one play and intercept a deep pass on the next. He was everywhere and he hit suddenly and without ceremony.

Carl didn't often play offense because he couldn't remember what to do on any given play. The coach would actually let him run the ball occasionally in a practice scrimmage, saying, "Just go straight ahead and Smith will get you the ball." We all knew that would be our goal-line offense if we needed it in a game. Carl could bull through a herd of rhinos. He didn't need to know where to go, other than "ahead." He would create his own path.

In practice or games, he'd always pick up his victim, dust him off and rapidly say something akin to, "Ni run, bid boy. You dot moves." Most of us simply couldn't make sense of his language when it was more than a one-word response, but I learned because I liked him from the first time he knocked my block off.

Carl had some serious challenges as a student. Most of the kids thought he was — in the language of the time — retarded. But I discovered him to be smart, perceptive, sensitive and always underestimated by teachers and students. He could barely read but in ret-rospect I guess that was his attention deficit or some-thing similar, a condition the medical community had not shared with us yet. It slowed him considerably, but it didn't keep him from living a full, healthy and good life as a husband, father, state champion football coach and hard-working provider in later years. Carl was one who would overcome, no matter the obstacle.

The hurdle on that Wednesday before Thanksgiving was finding a ride to Asheville, where my family lived. I was in a children's home in Banner Elk, living there for the year because my family wasn't working and didn't need another mouth to feed. Mom had her hands full and

Dad had died a couple of years earlier, leaving her and us nothing.

Carl and I would have to hitch-hike the 85 miles of winding mountain roads home and both of us had done enough thumbing for rides to have developed systems. We needed fresh haircuts because our near-Beatles shags were not in style in backwoods Avery County. It was important to wear clean, pressed jeans and shirts, leather shoes and, most important, our school letter jackets. Carl had a green one with a block "C" on the chest.

Our football coach had told me when I was brand new at Cranberry High that we only had one school color because we couldn't afford two. I thought he was pulling my leg, but later learned that it was true. A green and white uniform was cheap. A green and gold uniform cost $5 more. Avery was one of the poorest counties in America at the time and $5 was $5.

I had a black and gold letter jacket from the school where I had gone the year before. It was wool and leather with a block NA on the front for North Augusta High in South Carolina. We had won a state championship at my old school, so the jacket was nice, especially considering the white leather sleeves.

We both knew that the key to getting a ride was earning trust at a glance — the one the driver had of us in the seconds before he passed us. It was a science and Carl and I had developed our strategy well. We'd smile broadly, extend our arms with thumbs up and watch for brake lights as the car passed. Not many would fail to stop and take us a few miles. We might as well have been young girls pulling our skirts up above our knees.

Mom met us at the door after what seemed like a lightning trip from Cranberry to the center of Asheville where Mom lived with David, Paul and Becky. The rest of her eight kids were spread out over several states, working, going to college and me.

She slipped right past me to give Carl a deep and abiding hug. I got a "Hi, Danny." She was the last person on earth allowed to call me that. I said hello to the other kids and Carl interjected, addressing Mom, "I hungry. Got anyting eat?"

Mom looked at him, smiled and, mimicking Carl, said, "We dot tu-key. We dot gre-bean. We dot mash tata. We dot bi-kit. We dot I-tea, swee." Carl laughed out loud. Mom's irreverence charmed him and, as I mentioned, they understood each other.

Thirty minutes later, Carl and I pushed back from the table, ready to pop and burp at the same time. "Oh, dat gud," Carl said. "What fo Thank-givin?"

"You just ate it," said Mom, smiling. We had eaten a whole turkey.

Carl and I lounged the rest of the day, and into Thanksgiving morning. These were the first days of football season we'd been able to do that and we had one game left Friday night. The game against Mars Hill would be for the Appalachian Conference championship and a trip to the playoffs. That meant we needed to get our thumbs into the air late Thursday afternoon and hope for the best.

My young brother and sister, Becky and Paul, who were 10 and 11, clung to Carl like he was a brother returned from the wars. He played their games with them with genuine interest and their laughter filled the house.

I helped Mom prepare another turkey, which she had bought Wednesday evening as the store was closing, thinking she'd use her Social Security income from Dad's death. Dad's best friend owned a meat market and he gave her a real deal: free with trimmings ... and a smile.

We put on quite a feed and I was happy to be in the kitchen using the skills Mom had taught me. This was a lot of food and a rare treat for people unaccustomed to plenty. The "Ummmms" rang around the small dining room.

The kids and I cleaned the messy Thanksgiving table, giving Mom some time with Carl before we had to get on the road, and she seemed to appreciate it. Mom never declared much by way of affection, and she was not physically demonstrative, but we knew when she was content.

As Carl and I approached the front door to leave, Mom patted my back and looked at Carl. "Come here, boy," she said, throwing her arms wide to hug him. I would never have imagined that for one of her kids, but it seemed natural with Carl, who flooded the room again with his smile.

Five minutes later our arms were extended and our thumbs reached for the sky. A rusting Ford truck screeched to a stop on the side of Highway 19/25, just north of Asheville. We ran to catch it.

Veteran journalist Dan Smith is a member of the Virginia Communications Hall of Fame and author of eight books, including two novels, CLOG! and NEWS! He is an award-winning photographer as well. Among his many awards are the 2010 Virginia Business Journalist of the Year; a number of Virginia Press Association Awards for writing, photography and page design; awards for business ethics; environmental reporting; an Arts Council of the Blue Ridge award for literary contributions; two Perry F. Kendig awards for involvement in the arts, and others.

THE SAGA OF THE GREAT MAJESTIC

CELIA McCORMICK

When I bought my first wood burning cook stove, un-knowingly I also bought a century of images of rural life in the Blue Ridge mountains that filled my kitchen just as powerfully as the warmth of the "Great Majestic" itself.

I acquired the relic at an estate auction in late summer. It was one of those has-been picturesque farms, nestled in the foothills, whose inheritors had chosen to liquidate rather than maintain the old homeplace.

I felt like an intruder, who, like the other hundreds of bargain hunters, had invaded to capitalize on the bits and pieces of a rural family's heritage, parceled out to the highest bidders. Primitive wooden tools, the hand-crank meat grinder, cherry pitter and butter churn, the blue glass canning jars still filled with fruit, and the Great Majestic were reminiscent of an earlier, simpler life that few of us auction hawks could recall.

The legacy of my long sought after antique became clear as I dismantled the black cast iron monument. The scent of fresh pork sausage and buttermilk biscuits was as strong in the remaining ashes as if they'd been cooked that morning. The warming ovens above the range were sticky to the touch, as if honey and jam oozed out of a forgotten biscuit, left above for a warm mid-morning treat. The water tank adjacent to the wood-box was half full of water, ready to be heated for washing the next meal's dishes.

It took four men and me to move this heirloom from its stance. As I mustered every bit of strength in my hundred-pound frame, I became aware of at least one reason that rural life in the Blue Ridge remained immune to a growing transient society; I was reminded of this again later, as I pried away the door-jam of my back door to make way for the stove's entrance. It was obvious to me, at least, that when this stove moved in, a home was created around it and thoughts of ever moving again dissolved in smoke rings. There was little reason to move from these mountains, from a home where peach pits grew to blossoms and bore fruit for blue jars with zinc lids.

Each season with my stove carried its own ghosts of time past. It was as if the Great Majestic had a life of its own and invited me to share countless rituals in the company of unknown others.

During winter months, the stove worked full time, double shift, thanks to my middle-of-the-night stumblings to the kitchen to shake down the ashes and feed it a few chunks of wood, custom split to fit the small wood box. On snowy days it thawed my border collie, my toes, and my boot leather. Woolen mittens and socks took turns in the warming ovens. And from November to March, a pot of sassafras tea simmered perpetually on the back burner.

Chilly spring mornings were toasty until the noon sun was high and the wind laid, at which time the Great Majestic doubled as a charming antique, holding baskets of seed on their way to the garden and bouquets of sweet peas, daffodils and Queen Anne's lace.

Summer taught me the meaning of the old adage, "slaving over a hot stove," a sensation which no doubt inspired some inventor to design an alternative for canning summer's harvest. In autumn, the warmth was welcomed again. An earthen bowl of yeast bread rising in the warming ovens, herbs hanging to dry from the rafters above the stove, and a fresh pot of tea signaled another change of season.

The Great Majestic has moved only once since that late August day nearly 50 years ago; a creature of my generation, I have moved seven times. When the Great Majestic moved, a friend moved: a surrogate grandmother who prepared Thanksgiving dinner for what seemed like multitudes, practicing the ancient art of keeping it all bubbly and hot simultaneously; who comforted me on solitary winter nights; and who graced my house with an aura that radiated home like no other three-dimensional object I've ever owned.

The cook stove is someone else's treasure now and we have come full circle. For regardless of when and by whose hand it is fired again, I am now a part of the legacy of this great range. The aroma of my biscuits, the goo of my jam, and the melted rubber of my boot soles now belong to the Great Majestic.

Celia McCormick has lived in the Blue Ridge Mountains most of her life. After retiring from a career in adult and higher education, she's spent time gardening and appreciating the natural world. Having a collection of bits of paper with scribbled poems and memories collected since high school, she is now trying to organize these musings into a coherent written format. She has two daughters and four grandchildren.

THE CHRISTMAS THAT ALMOST WASN'T

DR. GRESILDA (KRIS) TILLEY-LUBBS

In the fall of 1950, the usual excitement and anticipation of the upcoming holiday season was suddenly dimmed. Mama was in the kitchen getting all the ingredients assembled for her famous chestnut and cornbread dressing when she gasped and grabbed the counter. She inched her way to the couch in the living room, bent almost double by the pain that wracked her body. I stood by her, crying and scared.

"Tillie," she called me by my childhood name, "go and get me the oil mop." I got her the floor dust mop as she asked, and then she got up and pushed her way into the nearby bathroom, leaning all her weight on the mop.

We were alone like that until my aunt Mary and uncle Paul showed up for the nightly trip over to my aunt Stella and uncle Kenneth's. They always came right after supper, and we all piled into Paul's red pick-up for the 20-minute trip from Oak Hill to Gatewood, West Virginia. But tonight, we didn't go anywhere. Mary just fixed us tomato soup and grilled cheese sandwiches. We ate some and waited for Daddy to get home from the coal mine where he worked the night shift. There was no phone to call the doctor. We would wait until morning, and then Daddy would take Mama to the doctor, who then would put her in the hospital. Mary and Paul would stay with me until my aunt Stella was able to come and pick me up so that I could stay with her and my uncle Kenneth while Mama was in the hospital.

At the time, I was four years old and didn't understand what was happening. Mama's attacks had become com-monplace since she was diagnosed the year before with undulant fever, the human version of brucellosis, a dis-ease that could destroy an entire herd of cattle in the blink of an eye. Although her health was never good, after that diagnosis, an attack of undulant fever could strike her down, sometimes resulting in her being in the hospital for a month or more.

Every year, Mama and my aunt Mary fixed Thanksgiving dinner for the "close family," the younger siblings of the 14 in their family. All the aunts, uncles, and cousins always gathered around Mary and Paul's big Cushman dining room table to enjoy the traditional Thanksgiving feast. That particular year, however, Mary fixed what she could, and we had Thanksgiving dinner, but the glow provided by Mama's special dressing and pumpkin pie was missing.

As Christmas drew closer, my longing for Mama to come home grew. My aunt Stella and uncle Kenneth loved me as the child they never had, but they weren't Mama. When I was born, Mama and Daddy took me home to the little two-room house beside Stella and Kenneth's, and Stella kept one ear cocked to come and take care of me when I cried in the night. Stella was my second mom, and their house was my other home where I spent days and weeks in their second bedroom, waiting for Mama to get well enough to come home.

The same uncles built both houses from Sears kits, but as much as I loved Stella, I still missed Mama. I missed the nights we spent playing canasta on the burgundy mohair velvet couch until midnight when Daddy got home. I missed reading with her and snuggling with her and Skipper, our red cocker spaniel. I missed my toys. I missed home. My four-year-old self longed to go home to the little house on Woods Avenue, in Oak Hill, West Virginia, that seemed another world from Gatewood and Stella and Kenneth's house.

Three days before Christmas Eve, Mama finally came home from the hospital, and Stella and Kenneth took me home to be with her. She was still weak and in excruciating pain. She spent her days on the couch, still using the oil mop to go to the bathroom, or to rustle up a little lunch for us. Despite her constant reassurance, my fear of losing her for good never left me. I carried my dolls and dollhouse into the living room to sit close to her. I carried my armloads of Golden Books so we could read together. Any time I left the living room, I worried about what I would find when I returned.

The worry I felt about Mama didn't compare to my sense of loss every time I looked at the empty spot in the corner of the living room where the Christmas tree should be glittering with lights and ornaments. There should be big red, green, blue, and yellow lights strung around the tree. Where were Grandaddy's ornaments? When I was six months old, my grandaddy died from a cerebral hemorrhage down in the mines before they could bring him up, and my grandma went into a deep depression. She vowed to never celebrate Christmas again, so as the oldest child, Daddy inherited all of Grandaddy's precious Christmas decorations, probably bought at the Brooklyn Company Store with the scrip the mines paid him that could be spent in the company store. Every Christmas, while she hung the ornaments on the tree, Mama told me how much Grandaddy loved Christmas, and how he would dance a jig around the tree when it was all decorated. Now his tinfoil garland and glass ornaments should be swinging on the branches next to my celluloid Santa and reindeer, and Rudolph the Red-Nosed Reindeer, and other childhood treasures. There was no angel that Mama and Daddy told me looked like me at the top of the tree. There were no presents under the tree that I could shake and guess the contents. My stocking wasn't lying on one of the presents waiting for Santa Claus to fill it.

This year, there was nothing. No tree. No lights. No ornaments. No packages. No stocking. Just the corner. It didn't even smell like Christmas with no pine scent coming from the tree and no good smells from cookies baking. Mama hadn't even made Grandma's special fruitcake recipe and wrapped it in whiskey-soaked flour sack towels.

Christmas Eve morning arrived, and I looked out the picture window at the gray sky and waited for the first snowflake to fall. I waited for a Christmas miracle. I waited for Santa Claus to sprinkle magic and make everything Christmas. In the afternoon, big heavy flakes started pouring from the sky. As twilight fell, Mama eased herself up from the couch and turned on the lamps just as the front door opened, and Stella and Kenneth came in, knocking the snow off of their boots.

Stella took off her coat and led me to my bedroom. She told me to put on the red and green dress she pulled out of the bag she was carrying. She helped pour me into my snowsuit, hat, mittens, and boots.

"Kiss your mama goodbye, and let's get going." Mama smiled at me and gave me the biggest hug ever.

Stella and Kenneth whisked me out of the door, one holding each hand. "Be careful on the steps," said Kenneth. "It's getting slick."

My glasses fogged up and got wet at the same time, but Stella and Kenneth led me safely to the blue Studebaker and tucked me in between them in the front seat.

Kenneth parked the car on Main Street. I looked at all the lights and people. There were even wreaths with candles hanging from the light poles. We got out of the car, and they took my hands again. They led me down the sidewalk to the Main Street Diner. I started jumping up and down when Kenneth opened the door and we went inside. I had never eaten in a restaurant!

After I ate my hamburger with fries, Stella bundled me back up in snowsuit, hat, mittens and boots, and we slipped and slid back to the car. Snow was still falling, and now it was piling up. The chains on the tires clanked and squeaked all the way back to the house on Woods Avenue.

As Kenneth parked in front of the house, I noticed a lot of cars — Mary and Paul's red pick-up, my aunt Lottie's black Studebaker, and my aunt Ruth and uncle Snooks' blue Chevy. My heart rose to my throat. Oh no! Had something happened to Mama? Stella and Kenneth held my hand firmly as we made our way up the six slick steps to the front door. When we opened the door, I couldn't believe my eyes. I saw the soft glow of colored lights.

"Santy Claus must have been here while we were gone!" Stella said as she smiled at my glistening eyes and open mouth.

And there it was! Magic!

The tree stood in the corner of the living room where it belonged. The lights shone and were reflected in the tinfoil garland and the tin cups that surrounded each light bulb. The ornaments sparkled. The presents were clustered close on the tree skirt, close to the tree trunk, to leave room for the new Lionel train chugging around the tree. My stocking was propped up on one of the presents with its telltale bulges for the orange and walnuts in the shell. Every year Mama reminded me that Santy Claus put an orange in her stocking and that was her big present in those depression years on the hardscrabble farm where she grew up. The scent of the orange mingled with the heady aroma of the pine tree. Plates were piled high with sugar cookies cut into Christmas tree and star shapes, gingerbread men, and peanut butter blossoms. Mary was in the kitchen pouring cups of hot chocolate and coffee. Mama lay back on the couch, looking weary but happy.

Daddy had come home early, and he had already taken a bath, so when he picked me up and held me in the air, he didn't smell damp like the mines. He held me high so I could put the angel on the top of the tree.

Christmas had come!

Dr. Gresilda (Kris) Tilley-Lubbs retired from Virginia Tech as Associate Professor Emerita of Second Language Education. After a career that focused on working with the Spanish-speaking community and preparing teachers to teach languages in schools, she now writes about her Appalachian roots deep in West Virginia coal country. She lives in Roanoke, Virginia, with her husband Dan. She has the good fortune of living in the same city as her three children and their families.

THE CHRISTMAS VEIL

LINDSEY SMITH HULL

"Stop your primping," Granny said, admonishing me as I tossed my locks over my shoulders in one of her only mirrors. It hung on her only closet door.

Mirrors meant bad luck, meant demons and devils and passing blood whispers, meant lightning balls and grim coverings when the moon dropped too low. Granny's religion was superstition served alongside wine and bread, hellfire and brimstone pickled in whiskey.

I was eight ... nine ... no more than eleven.

Primping was for fancy girls, Granny said, plaiting my hair as Grandmother Almond had plaited her own.

A lifetime ago, Granny had grown up, run away, danced amongst sailors, wrapped herself in glittering post-war gaiety, swirls of merry-making and beer-swilling and big-city living. For nearly forty years, she had managed a big-city Norfolk life.

The tiny apartment I knew brimmed with that same opulence. It contained few pocket cupboards to hide things away, and still, her archives contained a treasure trove of shiny-brite holidays. Especially Christmas.

Many decorations were handmade, stitched, glittered, though not all. Tinsel, angels, flickering window-candles to reflect my wide jack-frost morning-dew-eyes, jingle-bells and Santa-sleighs and reindeer-kisses, rickrack, aluminum, glazed, blushing innocence wrapped in Granny's soft pink negligee, dainty specimens of her peek-a-boo days.

Standing a foot and a half tall, Granny's tiny Tannenbaum sparkled in gold and silver, calling to girls turned out in hot pants dancing the evening-time waltz to Blue Christmas. Granny had wired shiny-brite-balls and ribbons to every branch, some no bigger than a rhinestone earring. Feathered aluminum looped around and around the diminutive conifer, a shimmery stole for winter's leading lady. It was Old Hollywood, it was Lana Turner, wrapped in fur.

Granny never took one ornament off those branches. At season's end, she wrapped it away and tucked it in its tiny dark cave.

The Granny I knew was a flat-footin', fried-chicken-cookin', foul-mouthed, hot-roller-and-knee-highs kind of on-her-own-woman. She told story after story about the Pamplin days — four brothers, three sisters, Mama and Daddy, and grandparents who lived 'round back on the tobacco farm. Granny's homespun tales splashed across my mind as readily as paint-with-water magic. She wasn't Appalachian; she was from Pamplin.

Granny was a puzzle piece that didn't quite fit, her loops and sockets crimped and mashed into sense. But across these mountains, our hearts beat the same. We sing the same high-country notes, tell the same tales three times over, have that same pick-me-up-and-try-me-again and it's-bound-to-happen-someday twang, pick the same sad harp and bouncing fiddle, play the same jump-the-fire blood-bound games.

Age six, I shimmied around my dad's Windy Gap living room, spinning and bouncing, joy bursting in my chest. I was near-the-mountainside, breeze blowing through box fans in every open window, freezer stocked with a rainbow of otter pops.

Alvin and the Chipmunks' sing-song voices blended with my own, filling the room with wishes of toy planes and hula hoops, their Christmas album spinning on Daddy's old record player. I bounced along — the burnt sienna-striped couch my personal stage, my yowling kitten Sam my best back-up singer.

Daddy kept the beat out on the front porch, stomping Virginia clay off his combat boots. He'd be in soon.

Alvin and I belted out the next song, ready to ring the bells, to deck the halls. The screen door opened, then slapped shut.

"What're you up to?" Daddy asked. He grinned his silly grin at me, his arms full of fresh picked tomatoes and cucumbers, straight off the vine.

"Merry Christmas!" I shrieked, my little bounces growing higher and higher into hops, jumps. "Let's hang the lights!"

Daddy held out his hands to calm me, then joined in my singing. "Alvinnnnnnnn!" he shouted with me when the time was right. Sam scatted.

Daddy had spunk; he also had too many closets to look through. We weren't going to hang lights that summer day. It would take too long to find the right box, he said.

Christmas could live all year long in our hearts, he told me, with or without the decorations.

When Christmastime did come around, Daddy always made sure we had a tree. He said a friend gave him this artificial thing way before they became popular [read cheap], which meant that one of his electrical clients had probably passed it on, or that he'd found it at the fancy thrift shop. When it came time to set up that tree, we had to stick every individual branch on the middle stem, in precisely the right color-coded order. Then we'd fluff that spindly baby as much as we could — I'd seen that part on tv.

The tree wasn't pre-lit, never heard of such a thing. His lights were a mix of colored and white. Some flashing, some not, and not one ever flashed on the same schedule. The simple box of glass and string balls was very different from Mama's collection. He just had red, green, and white orbs, no characters or refrains from the past. I liked it that way.

And the icicles. Metallic streamers dangled from every branch of the tree. Some folks lobbed handfuls of tinsel at the tree like haphazard cranks. I delicately placed one lock after the other, my tree a queen preparing for her coronation.

When I was nine, Daddy moved to a mountain house in a real mountain hollow. This one day, Daddy grabbed a saw and we went hiking, pulling my sled behind.

Ten minutes from the house, we found a Christmas tree. It looked a lot like someone else's Christmas tree, that had maybe been planted there a few years before. I was suspicious, insisting that that was not our tree.

We walked to the top of the next hill, and Daddy grew tired of the game.

I convinced him to climb one more hill. There, two trees stood side by side. One was tall-like-Daddy and spindly. The other was short-and-fat, more a my-height-bush than a tree.

Both trees went home with us, stood tall-or-short in the wood-paneled living room, decorated and watered the whole season through. Their pine needles dropped but their branches stood strong.

"Mom collects Christmas trees," my son told his fiancé last October, discussing their own holiday decor. "The attic is full of them."

This is true. I keep them in a small attic closet. The short squat door mirrors Granny's closet portal. The long narrow room is a hiding place for treasures.

One tree tall, two trees small, ceramic for the curio top, a blo-mold for the porch. Homemade goes up the stairs, white for vintage-air, and our initial three-footer is always put to good use. And tinsel. Cue the tinsel, stage right.

Mama liked the smell of a good old pine tree. She always wanted a fresh one, cut from the farm. Sometimes we'd go to a lot, driving to the mall or to the hardware store. We lived in Roanoke City, on the cusp of the county. We could get anywhere within fifteen minutes, twenty if we lost our way.

Oftentimes, though, we'd go up the mountain. That meant a longer drive, but Mama loved it. Her Uncle

Lacey had driven her all over Virginia when she was little, into West Virginia and Kentucky, too, she said. Our drives reminded her of those good times; he was like her dad.

On we'd go, my stepdad driving, my stomach knotting up through the turns. Up Bent Mountain, all the way to Floyd, through Hillsville, even. I'd keep pointing out trees and still we wouldn't stop.

It was called Slaughter's Tree Farm, near Fancy Gap — I remembered, Daddy had brought me here, just once. A little white shack, green wreath, red bow. Trees ... they lined up in rows upon rows on either side of that tidy, hedged drive. They stretched out, and they stretched, and they stretched as far as my eye could see. Every obedient fir quietly standing in place. Embroidered trinkets, whipped stitches.

We walked far, me desperately trying to keep up with my stepdad's too-long legs. Ticking at the metronome in my head: keep up, keep up, keep up.

Mama pointed; he chopped all life out of the perfect specimen, round on all sides, just so tall. A whatever-you-wanted-it-to-be fir. A yes-sir.

Candy-striped evergreen farmers laced that sucker up like any ordinary day. We all gathered around the fire. A bourgeois display.

Mama kept memories bound up in furniture, antiques. Arriving home, she'd insist on rearranging things before anything else could come in the door.

My stepdad would have to trim the tree before the tree could be trimmed. Because that six-foot-evergreen? It was eight-feet, ten. Mama would know if he knocked it off the top, so he'd have to take it off the bottom, make sure everything was clean. By the time it was done, my stepdad would have said — at least a hundred times — that he was never buying a live one again.

The tree came through the tight squish of a too-narrow door, straight in the kitchen, and through to the sitting room. Needles shook off all over Mama's perfect tamped-down mauve carpet. Into the stand. Down again, up again. Three times or four, until that tree could stand tall and straight, Mama's pride. Her Christmas tree.

She made herself busy, weaving thousands of colorful lights through its limbs, lighting the tree to excess — every one of those lights matched perfectly. The garland a prismatic boa, fluffed-out and full, a fat-cat's rainbow-permed tail. Lazily, it bowed across the fullness of the tree's branches, swags shimmering in a full display of Kodachromatic brilliance.

Mama's production continued as she carefully paraded through the rooms with coffers of mismatched ornaments, some heirloom, some Hallmark, some handmade with my fingerprints, cut-outs, glue-sticks, tin. Tightly, she oversaw my placement of every one.

If I dropped a ball ... heaven forbid.

Granny knew loss. She loved hard, married, and ran. How she ran, steaming a one-way track to Norfolk, alone. Fifteen years down the line, pink ribbons ran through those same hard-nosed lines, impossible fairways for fair maidens. A Christmas favor from one sibling to another.

Family ticked away, blue-lined script returned to sender, obituaries spelled in hit and run. The luck runs bad when your heart pumps tobacco, aces, and whiskey.

She passed in 94, an Almond turned a Clark.

I fell ill, eleven, had thought Granny never would ever let me go.

Mama went to my primping mirror and opened that closet door. She took Granny's little tree and tucked it away, saved it in a box for another day. Said it would be okay. Christmas trees last forever.

Years later, Mama said, Granny's tree fell to dust. She sent it to the dump.

I've wrapped Granny's feathered tinsel around my heart, poked the aluminum into every sore and bound myself in every loose end.

I tucked Mama's Kodachrome swag and Daddy's icicle angel hair in nooks and crannies that bled with blood-root tears, the hallowed wails that poured forth the eve I left to wander through Slaughter's midnight balsam firs. I drew and wrenched and twisted every strand tighter than tight, as tight as wind-up-soldier's spring can ever get, hoping to heal.

No matter how hard I pulled those strings, I never could find another Christmas that glowed like Granny's glitz and glamor.

I crawled through that too-low door, into my treasured Christmas-tree cove, into that too-narrow space like that space before. I bawled and I bawled all the tears I was never allowed to heal, and I curled my heart around myself and waited under my bourgeois collection of fluffed-out firs, staring hard into Granny's gilded primping mirror, just like she would have stared as she passed by.

Those rabble-house, tobacco-growing, card-rousing, whiskey-barrel Almonds ... they lined up in rows upon rows of tidy hedged fields and they marched forth, and they marched, and they marched, and they marched right into me.

Except Granny.

She always said that the veil was thinnest when our hearts were squeezed too tightly.

I squeezed again.

Lindsey Smith Hull has always begged people to tell her stories. Now, she collects those tales as a freelance journalist, essayist, and poet. Hull was selected as Roanoke's 2024 Writer by Bus; her resulting chapbook, a debut poetry collection entitled the mountains rumble, was released in September 2024.

THE DAY OF THE DEAD IN VIRGINIA

AMANDA COCKRELL

There is something about late October that pulls the curtains apart and leaves us staring into mystery. The leaves whirl around our heads in a mindless dance, carried on a wind that electrifies the cats' fur so that they also run a little mad. No wonder so many different cultures have marked this cross-quarter day, midway between the fall equinox and the winter solstice, as a hinge point in the year, when anything might visit from the other side.

In October we start to think of the Ancestors, and those more recently lost, still beloved, still remembered, and because we are transplanted Southern Californians, we look homeward for the way to greet them, offering marigolds and the scent of chilies and chocolate.

The Day of the Dead is celebrated in Mexico and much of the U.S. Southwest on November 1 and 2 as El Día de Los Muertos, and has now arrived in Roanoke with an influx of folk from Mexico, but our personal celebration of it is decades old, a comforting family ritual of remembrance. The dates coincide with All Saints Day and All Souls Day of the Christian calendar, but this tradition is older, with its origins among the Aztecs. On those turning-of-the-year days, when the borders between the worlds are thin, those who have gone through the door to the next world may come back to visit.

The children, los angelitos, arrive first, on November 1, followed by the adults. Graveyards are spruced up and flower-bedecked. Houses are decorated with skeleton figures and sugar skulls to remind us that death is just another world. Families make altars where they place the things that the departed loved. Candy for los angelitos, cigars and whiskey for the old men. I find myself shopping for them in October the way I shop for the living in December.

The heart of the Day of the Dead is the ofrenda, the altar with pictures of our lost loved ones, and little gifts for them to enjoy. Chocolate and gin and a china dog for my mother. Bourbon for my father, and a good poker game with old pals. For my daughter, photos of the late pugs. The pugs were her fault, sort of. She longed for one and we finally gave in. Three more accreted somehow, so I'll put their pictures and some dog biscuits on the altar for her, beside the miniature purse I bought at Target. Brandy for my father-in-law, and his slide rule from the corner cabinet in the living room. Scotch for my ex-husband, to say, "I know it really wasn't all your fault."

I like to think they appreciate it. Certainly, they tell me stories. No one has more stories than the dead. "Remember the gardener who was so good with roses," they whisper in my ear. "Remember when he shot his wife's back-door man and all the rose growers in town put the arm on the judge?" And I do. I remember as if I had been there. "Remember Cousin Willetta?" they murmur, and I recall the family lottery of who-would-drive-Willetta, because Willetta didn't drive, and listen to her complain for hours that no one could fit a shoe properly these days because she bought fives when she needed sixes. She was a sod widow and her sister was a grass widow and they lived together with six cats and made dreadful jam.

My husband's grandfather is there too, handsome and feckless, who sang for eight hours on a bet and never repeated a song. His wife stumps along behind him, a woman not to be trifled with, so tough that when he died, everyone called her Pa. They all come to visit, the newly lost a comfort to think of again, the distant ones just a nod through the wavy glass of the front window, their hands full of history.

It's time to bake too, for the dead and for our friends, and the annual party we throw to remember our dead and theirs. Tamales, and empanadas, and Pan de Muertos and chocolate skulls, because the Day of the Dead isn't a timid holiday. It's the day we remember that we are all bones under the skin, all dancing into the next world. The kitchen is full of chilies, and beer to go with it while we stir. Coriander for healing, and cinnamon for love and lust. Chilies are a charm against spells, important when the doors stand open to other worlds, but also for fidelity.

We'll fill vases with marigolds, little bright flowers of the dead, and calla lilies for the Virgin and for rebirth. We'll unpack the sugar skulls and art accumulated through the years; put the skeletons, Catrina and El Jefe, on the porch, satin finery over their papier-mâché bones, so the spirits know they're welcome. I've always thought of this party as a living entity, a hive spirit composed of the rotating cast of friends who come each year, bringing marigolds and bottles of wine and pictures of their own for remembrance when the leaves are turning, scuttering across the yard with the wind behind them, and the borders between the worlds are transparent.

No one is sure when the dead arrive at the party, but they do, unseen, in a breath of ginger cologne, a rustle of silk, a small warm wind. The Day of the Dead welcomes these returning souls, says to them, "Come in, have a drink, smoke a cigar, remember how we still love you. You are our own. Who are you that we should fear you?"

Amanda Cockrell is the author of Are You Now or Have You Ever Been?, a novel of the Hollywood blacklist. Her other works include Coyote Weather, a novel of the Vietnam War years, and the young adult novel What We Keep Is Not Always What Will Stay. As Damion Hunter she also writes Roman era historical adventure. She is the former director of the Children's Literature graduate program at Hollins University. https://www.amandacockrell.com/

Founder's Day

Josh Urban

Long Mountain lives up to its name, stretching a blue wall above the rolling hills, the last outpost in the east, the guardian. It watches me trudge through the hay field, out of the locust and poplar shade, past the bees drifting in and out of their hives, then skirt the chattering sprinkler watering a tender lawn still under straw. This land will get into your bones. The whippoorwill sings every year, and your heart will break along with his, if you listen. Sometimes you'll know why, and sometimes you won't, but it always will when he sings late by the creek.

The sun drenches Long Mountain and invites me for an afternoon reverie. Mountains and sunshine will do that, you know.

I'm new here, and I'm not. The mountains have called forever. When I was a boy, the family would camp in the heights. The smell of a campfire brings me back in an instant. When I was a young man, the blue hills would beckon through the haze of the city. There's one rise in the concrete raceway where they first appear fifty miles to the west, even through the smog and the insanity of twelve lanes.

"I'm going scouting," I said one day, although it wasn't a surprise. Two hours into the trip, my brand new car blew a transmission. The dealer asked if I had an appointment. "No, no, nobody was expecting me, but I limped it back here."

The loaner car fared better, summiting the mountains south of Charlottesville, and rolling past the blooming redbud in the gauzy spring. It's everywhere.

There's a spot on 29 south where the emptiness is profound. Panic rushed into the void. What am I doing, leaving the city behind? But the car rolled on. More redbud bloomed in a town, gracing the parking lot. Time seemed slower. A stranger answered when I spoke, answering a question I didn't ask, and then I knew. I could be happy here. Even the red bricks were mellow in that fragile warmth of early spring.

To the west, and to more vistas, more emptiness, more granite and limestone and redbud contending with the crags, bursting forth in a joyous symphony of color among the ancient gray.

I could be happy here a hundred times over.

The on-ramp is always nearby, especially for a city boy, the red, white, and blue sign pointing to fast times and the blur of speed. I called my dad from the interstate, on my way back to the maze of asphalt where mountains are only an abstraction. "You should see it out here. Redbud everywhere." I was sold.

The stories of the old pioneers tickle my fancy: how they had to undergo a dying of sort, to leave it all behind, hewing a path through the wilds to found a new life. We still travel those roads, but we don't pay attention to the first unseen hands. Maybe it's because we need all of our concentration for the hairpin turn in an Appalachian rainstorm. Or maybe it's because we forgot.

My voyage is different, modern, easier, although I'd like to build something as lasting as one of those licorice roads. So I came to Long Mountain and built a house, and now the sprinkler brings me back to the present with a gentle splash of sweet cool water. I look around and smile. It's good here, a place to make something grow. Summer brings the green shade of the sassafras. (Maybe I'll learn to brew root beer this year.) Autumn lights the mountain on fire, and Winter offers a blanket of cloud for a hibernation. But each spring, when the redbud blooms, it's a reminder of that season when the car worked and the mountains sang me home. I could be happy here.

When the redbud blooms, it's Founder's Day. And I am.

Josh Urban is a writer, storyteller, and musician. He's the author of Cities on a Hill, The Captain's Logbook, and the upcoming Early Work. Urban has written for Sky and Telescope, Astronomy and other magazines, pens a weekly syndicated column, publishes The Nighthawk newsletter for a regional senior citizen audience, and maintains an active blog .

REDISCOVERING THE WONDER OF CHRISTMAS

WAYNE JORDAN

Christmas evokes nostalgia in many of us. Our emotions may be roused by the soft glow of twinkling lights or memories of gathering around the family table. Other times, financial stress, emotional strain, or family tensions cloud the celebration. For many, the luster of the season has become tainted. There's little joy to be found. The wonder of Christmas has vanished.

But here's the thing: there's still wonder to be found. Beneath the stress, to-do lists, and financial worries, Christmas traditions can reconnect us to something profound. Whether you celebrate the holiday with religious observances or love the season for its warmth and nostalgia, wonder is still there. But finding it can be challenging.

I admit to having lost my sense of Christmas wonder for a time. But I'm happy to report that I have rediscovered it. Or perhaps it rediscovered me.

As a kid, Christmas was pure magic — the lights, the decorations, the excitement of gifts under the tree. I couldn't wait for the day. When I hit my twenties, Christmas was a stream of holiday parties and socializing. Then came parenthood — and I acquired a new set of eyes. Watching my kids light up at the sight of a Christmas tree or hearing their laughter as they tore into their presents brought some wonder back into Christmas.

But as the years rolled on, my attitude about the holiday changed. Lethargy set in. I'd heard the same Christmas carols ad nauseam. I could recite the biblical Christmas story in my sleep. Shopping and socializing became burdens. I was bored with it all. I'd just as soon stay home and read a book.

Then, a few years ago, I had an epiphany. Christmas wonder returned, stirred by a simple Appalachian hymn. I was in a coffee house, surrounded by people, conversations, clanging dishes, and shuffling feet. Friends greeted one another with warm hugs and expressions of love. A pair of musicians performed on the stage: two lovely voices accompanied by mountain dulcimer and classical guitar. The duo mainly played Christmas standards: God Rest Ye Merry Gentlemen, The First Noel, and others.

Then they played I Wonder as I Wander. I'd heard it before but never really listened. The song felt different that day, as if speaking directly to me. Maybe the gentle, waltz-like rhythm or the haunting minor key crept into my thoughts unawares.

The music caused the word wonder to echo in my mind. I realized then that I had stopped looking for wonder in Christmas. I had been so caught up in the holiday hustle that I had ignored the details: a song, a lighted candle, the aroma of a freshly cut Christmas tree, the feel of crisp winter air on my face. Even the din of downtown shopping held a certain charm.

With the realization that I had lost my Christmas wonder, I recognized an emotional emptiness in my breast. It was a tender spot, pleading to be filled. What could I do to recapture the feeling? The answer became self-evident.

I Wonder as I Wander spoke to me. It filled the hollow in my breast. The hymn I Wonder as I Wander captured the heart of that feeling — wonder. The song speaks to anyone who has paused to reflect on the mystery of life. The lyrics express a quiet yearning for understanding, a curiosity transcending religion. This is why the song resonates deeply, even for those who do not religiously celebrate Christmas. It's about seeking answers, finding peace, and feeling connected to something larger than ourselves — things we all crave, especially during the holiday season.

My curiosity was piqued: Where did this hauntingly beautiful hymn come from? Like the song, the answer is rooted in simplicity and wonder, starting in a small Appalachian town. It's fitting that this song emerged from the Appalachian hills — a region often marked by poverty but rich in culture and tradition. The song's modest origins reflect the essence of Christmas itself, a holiday that, at its best, is about finding joy and wonder in simple things.

I Wonder as I Wander wasn't born out of a grand cathedral or penned by a famous composer. Instead, it emerged from far humbler roots. It began with a few simple lines sung by a young girl — Annie Morgan — in the town square of Murphy, North Carolina, during the summer of 1933. The scene wasn't glamorous. Annie and her father, an itinerant preacher, had been living in the town square — squatting, really — much to the displeasure of the locals. They had been holding daily revival meetings but had overstayed their welcome.

With tensions high and a threat of being forced out, Annie's father begged the town to allow him to hold one more revival meeting. He hoped to collect enough donations to buy gas and move on. And it was during that last revival, with the dust of the streets swirling in the hot July air, that Annie sang those first three haunting lines of I Wonder as I Wander. Unwashed but undeniably beautiful, her voice echoed through the square, carrying the quiet yearning and wonder that would later touch hearts far beyond that mountain town.

In attendance at that meeting was John Jacob Niles, a folklorist who journeyed through the mountains, searching for songs rooted in the Old World but re-shaped by Appalachian culture. Fascinated by the young girl and the tune, Niles asked her to sing it to him. Each time she did, he paid her 25 cents. After eight tries, each carefully transcribed by Niles, only the melody and three lines of verse were captured. From those scant beginnings, Niles shaped the hymn we know today.

The wonder of Christmas can be found in many places, but for me, it came through music. I Wonder as I Wander reignited something I thought had faded. Could it do the same for you? Maybe. But the truth is, it doesn't have to be this specific hymn. Any Christmas carol or hymn has the power to evoke wonder if we truly listen. The right song, at the right moment, can open your eyes to the beauty and mystery of the season.

Take Silent Night. Its humble origins — a small church in Austria and a broken organ — are far removed from the song's lasting impact. Yet its simple melody and peaceful lyrics invite reflection. Everything slows down when you hear it in the stillness of a candlelit church or softly playing in the background on Christmas Eve. The noise fades, and a sense of calm and awe remains.

Or consider O Holy Night, with its powerful notes and stirring message. The grandeur of the music draws you in, but the heartfelt plea of the lyrics — "Fall on your knees!" — stirs something deeper. Those words make you pause, inviting reflection whether you're religious or not.

Christmas music transcends the commercial chaos that often overshadows the season. It calls us back to something simple and pure. Whether it's a choir in a grand cathedral or a lone singer in a small-town square, the wonder is there if you're willing to listen.

So this year, as the holidays approach, take a moment to truly listen. Let familiar or new music remind you of the wonder and enchantment that's still there. In the quiet moments beneath all the distractions, you may find the peace and connection that make Christmas truly special.

Wayne Jordan is a writer and storyteller based in Galax. His Scots-Irish ancestors settled in the Blue Ridge Mountains in 1760, and he has deep roots here. The author of four books, Wayne is a retired Senior Editor for WorthPoint Corporation, a long-time columnist for the magazine Kovels Antique Trader, and a contributor to regional newspapers and travel publications. He blogs at blueridgetales.com

REVIEW

Thank you for reading Appalachian Holidays.

We hope it adds joy to your holiday season. If you enjoyed this collection, we would love to hear from you. Please leave us a review on Amazon, Facebook, or wherever you purchased this book. Your feedback and support are important to us.

Now go out there and have a beautiful holiday – wherever you are.

Made in the USA
Middletown, DE
17 January 2026